About the author

Matthew Rawlins was born in Wolverhampton and is a graduate of the National Film and Television School. He is an award-winning creative director, screenwriter, novelist and dad.

Cover illustration by Poppy Tshaya Kay.

OSCAR AND HIS SPECTACULAR SPECTACLES

Matthew Rawlins

OSCAR AND HIS SPECTACULAR
SPECTACLES
THE MYSTERY VICTORY

Vanguard Press

A CIP catalogue record for this title is
available from the British Library.

ISBN 978-1-784655-81-5

Vanguard Press is an imprint of
Pegasus Elliot MacKenzie Publishers Ltd.
www.pegasuspublishers.com

First Published in 2020

Vanguard Press
Sheraton House Castle Park
Cambridge England

Printed & Bound in Great Britain

Dedication

For the most 'Spectacular' boys in the world, Jude and Oscar. My constant source of love and inspiration.

Chapter One
Oscar

Oscar was an ordinary boy. He lived with his mum, dad and his dog, who he had named Watson after one of his heroes, Dr Watson, from the Sherlock Holmes stories. He thought this suited his dog as he was particularly good at finding things. If you hid food anywhere, for example, Watson would find it within seconds, much like Watson and his friend, Holmes, found clues to solve crimes.

Oscar liked many things, just like other boys: bugs, chocolate, football and farts. Farts always made him laugh, unless Watson did them after eating a big bone, then he didn't laugh, those farts made his eyes water even if he held his nose.

The thing he liked the most though were detective stories. His passion for tales of detection had come about because of his father's job; he was a policeman, a real-life detective. Oscar didn't get to see him that much because he had to work so hard in the city solving crimes, catching crooks, protecting the Queen, eating doughnuts. Oscar worried that because his dad was away all the time there was no one at home to solve the local crimes. He also worried that he ate too many doughnuts and smoked too many cigarettes.

Oscar asked his dad one night, "How do you know the difference between the truth and a lie?" thinking this must be pretty important when trying to catch a criminal.

His father replied, "The truth is sometimes hard to say, but always easy to see, if you look hard enough."

Oscar thought he was OK then; he could easily become a detective as he had very good eyesight. He could watch the TV sitting right back on the sofa, not like his friend, Luke, who sat smack bang in front of the screen. His mum said he would get square eyes, but he never did. That was just one of those things mums said, like, 'If the wind changes you'll stick like that!' but that wasn't true either.

Saying all of that, recently Oscar had started having to squint to see the television. Sometimes he got headaches.

"Why are you squinting?" quizzed his mum one night after he had been allowed up late to watch *Doctor Who*. Oscar lied and said he wasn't squinting, merely concentrating, as he quickly tried to straighten out the frown lines on his forehead. His dad lowered his paper, peered over the top suspiciously, only for a moment, then raised it back up. It was the look Oscar imagined his dad gave the criminals he caught just before he said, "You're nicked!"

When he finally confessed about the headaches, his mum said that maybe they should pay a visit to the optician. Oscar looked up 'optician' on his dad's computer. It was a word only whispered in a hushed tone, a bit like 'the dentist' or 'he who must not be named' from the Harry Potter books. Nobody wanted to wear glasses, have big braces on their teeth or have the world's most evil wizard hunting you down. *It's the end of the world,* thought Oscar.

The computer screen filled with images of scared people with space helmet-looking things strapped to their heads, metal glasses so big you would need a couple of people just to pick them up.

Every image that appeared made him more and more uneasy; it looked like wearing glasses was pretty much the same as medieval torture.

He thought about all of the detectives he admired; none of them wore glasses: hats, raincoats, a lot of cool jackets, but no glasses. *Detectives don't wear glasses because then they wouldn't be able to see the truth*, he thought.

Oscar's mum rang every optician in the area to try and get an appointment for an eye test but, for some reason or another, no one had any availability, at least not for another week. She was about to give up when the phone rang.

It was an optician.

To be precise, it was the secretary of a Mr Rouse of Rouse Opticians. Oscar's mum was very confused, she didn't remember a Rouse on the list, but assumed that it must have been one of the numbers that she had rung earlier.

It wasn't. Mr Rouse was a very special optician. Something quite out of the ordinary, in fact he was spectacular.

Chapter Two
The Failed Dodge

"Oscar!" shouted his mum up the stairs.

She had looked everywhere for him; they were going to be late for Mr Rouse. "We need to go…now!"

She had looked around the house for him but hadn't thought to look in Oscar's wardrobe, because she hadn't realised just how much her son was dreading his visit to the opticians. He told her whilst he was cleaning his teeth the previous night that he wasn't at all keen on wearing glasses, but she had missed the look of sheer terror in his eyes.

"Let's just see what happens hey?"

"But what if I can't 'see'?" Oscar said, blinking furiously to check his eyes were still working.

The only other boy who wore glasses in his class was Ben Mullett, and he smelt like cheese. Not cheese you wanted to eat, spread on a cracker or sprinkle on your spag bol, but foot cheese.

"I don't want to go!" he whispered to Watson, who was also hiding in the wardrobe. The dog had other things on his mind. He didn't care about going to the optician; he needed a wee. He started to whine and shuffle his bum.

"Quiet Watson! Stay still!" Oscar yanked a jumper off a hanger and dropped it on Watson's head.

Oscar heard the squeak of the bedroom door as it opened. Through the slim crack in the wardrobe door he watched his mum get down on her knees and look under the bed. Watson whined again. It was muffled by the jumper but enough for Oscar's mum to discover their hiding place. There was no escape.

Oscar sat staring out the window; he liked it the most when it was raining and he could watch the droplets race each other across the glass. His mum had only just started letting him sit in the front. Most of his friends still had to sit in the back, but he had heard his older cousin, Jon, shout the word 'shotgun' each time he got near a car, and he always got to sit in the front.

That was the key. He heard from someone else that you could also say 'bagsy'. When he asked his cousin about which one was the best to use, he said that 'bagsy' was the law even more than shotgun, he just chose shotgun because it sometimes made people duck when they heard it. Oscar asked his dad if you could get arrested for ignoring a 'bagsy'. His dad said that it was just one of those rules.

Oscar found some rules confusing, but he thought he would give this one a try. For a couple of weeks he shouted 'bagsy' each time he got near the car until his mum let him sit in the front after one of his shouts shocked Mrs Reid, next door, so much she accidentally cut off the head of one of her prize roses.

Oscar's mum was listening to Elton John's *Rocket Man* again. He moaned about her playing it over and over but it was actually one of his favourite songs, mainly because he could imagine Elton flying around space in his star-shaped glasses singing to the aliens. He was hoping the optician would have something similar. They were the only glasses he had ever seen that he liked.

Watson was on the back seat. He had come under the guise of offering moral support, but really he was along for the ride because he was sure he had lost a biscuit under the driver's seat. He could smell something, but then again Mum never really cleaned the car out so it could have just been an abandoned banana skin or something.

"How come you don't wear glasses?" Oscar asked his mum. She wasn't sure what to say at first; she didn't want him to think it was a problem in any way.

"I just don't suit them really," she eventually replied.

Oscar knew that it wasn't just a 'style' issue. He could smell a cover up; his mum always cleared her throat when she was lying. His dad clicked his knuckles if he was trying to hide the truth and Watson burped when he was trying to cover his tracks.

Oscar's eyes had stopped working and that was all there was to it. *What would be next?* he thought in panic. He wiggled his toes and his fingers; they were still working, for now. His nan had told him it was silly to worry, but then he just worried he was being silly.

It was a family tradition that when Oscar went to the dentist, he always got a Star Wars figure as a reward. He was attempting to build an army of Stormtroopers and had hatched a plan to eat as many sweets as possible. He even started drinking tea just so he could have a spoonful of sugar in it, in the hope that he would need to see the dentist every week.

He was thinking the optician might be a similar opportunity; you book an appointment, sit in a chair, get told something is wrong with you and then leave feeling worse than you did when you arrived. On the upside, if you played along, you usually got something out of it, even if it was just a magazine or some football stickers.

He thought he would try his luck and offered up the dentist comparison to his mum, stating that it was only fair if he played ball, made no fuss, that he should be rewarded. Mum said he could if he behaved, listened and said please and thank you. Watson barked. He thought he probably deserved something too for coming along.

"Yes Watson, you can have a treat too," she said.

Chapter Three
The Perfect Fit

The optician was housed in a strange building. It was one of those concrete blocks that looked like the government had once used it to keep secrets. It was square and concrete with lots of high fencing round the perimeter and mirrored windows to stop anyone looking in. The whole place was one giant pair of sunglasses.

The hanging sign outside was a big pair of metal glasses with one winking eye. Or maybe it was squinting? It was definitely watching him; Oscar moved his head from side to side and, sure enough, the big plastic eyes followed him.

The reception was much like a doctor's waiting room. Oscar was surprised that there weren't any glasses on display. There were some old toys in the corner that his mum nodded to as they walked in. Oscar frowned; he thought he was way too old to play with those kinds of toys but, eventually, the call of the spiral marble run was too much and he sauntered over there as casually as he could. His mum leafed through one of the dusty, donated magazines with pictures of furniture and smiling people.

Watson had to stay in the car, but he didn't care, it was the perfect opportunity to find the mystery biscuit treasure he thought he had caught a whiff of. His hunt for the treat led him to an old, half-chewed sweet that had gone particularly gooey in the heat and was now firmly lodged in his back teeth. No matter how hard he tried, he just couldn't get rid of it.

He cursed the fact that he didn't have fingers.

Oscar had just worked out how to race two marbles at the same time when he was distracted by the site of a peculiar looking man standing in the reception, as if he had appeared out of thin air. He was a little bit like Yoda, although he didn't have pointed ears or, for that matter, green skin. It was more in the way he spoke, kind of back to front, and the way his funny little fingers busied themselves adjusting his half-moon glasses to read the notes in front of him. Oscar wondered if the real Yoda had to wear glasses to read the Star Wars scripts and just took them off when they were filming. He also wondered why an optician would have to wear glasses at all.

"Oscar Chesterton?" the funny man called out, eventually looking up over the top of his notepad and perusing the reception area. Oscar and his mum perused with him. It was pretty obvious he was Oscar Chesterton as there was nobody else in there, except for the bored looking goldfish, tired looking Power Rangers and weary houseplants.

Oscar waited for his mum to acknowledge the man in the hope that if he didn't say anything, sat totally still, then maybe he could just slip out unnoticed. It seemed as though the man who looked like Yoda couldn't see very well anyway, which, when Oscar thought about it a bit more, was quite worrying. After all, he was meant to be the eye doctor.

Once they walked through the door that led out from the back of the reception, they seemed to walk for hours. They turned left, right, left, right again and again. At points they even seemed to turn back on themselves. They went up two flights of stairs, in a lift and then strolled across a very pleasant garden where Oscar was sure they were being watched by someone or something lurking in the dark green shadowy corners. Each time they thought they had arrived, the little man would beckon them on further with his hand, apologising repeatedly and saying simply, "Nearly there, just up here, this way."

The walk was so epic that Oscar's mum said she wished she had worn a different pair of shoes for the occasion. Oscar wondered if anyone had ever got lost on the way to an appointment. He was half expecting to bump into some poor lost soul, clothes torn and tattered like a 'Robinson Crusoe' type or a Count from one of his Musketeer books, abandoned and forgotten in a dank, dark cell, shackled to the wall by chains. But they didn't see anyone, not a soul.

There were hundreds of doors, all of them closed.

On one occasion, when the little man stopped to catch his breath and wipe the sweat from the lenses of his glasses, Oscar rested himself up against the nearest door. He could have sworn he heard the click-clack of machinery accompanied by hushed voices whispering away in some sort of coded language, a bit like the Morse Code he had learned about at school. His inquisitive brain was desperate for him to burst through the door and find out what was really going on, but just as his fingertips touched the door handle they were off again and the strange noises faded into the distance as they moved on.

Eventually, they stopped in front of one of the doors. It had a large shiny bronze plaque at the top that was engraved with; 'Mr Rouse, Optometrist.' followed by a long list of letters with dots between them. He was obviously very important. The old man tut-tutted as he took a moment to wipe a smudge from the brass.

It was relatively dark inside the room except for a light on the wall that had what looked like the alphabet on it. But it wasn't in the same order as the alphabet that Oscar knew, and some letters were smaller than others. Some were so small they almost disappeared, like little ants running off the bottom of the screen.

Oscar assumed that he would be made to read the letters as they were positioned on the wall directly in front of a large, ominous black chair facing them. It was a bit like the chair he recognized from his numerous trips to the dentist, but there was something more sinister about this one.

The chair was raised on a steel platform but there was no little bowl at the side that you spat pink stuff into and no big light hanging above it. Instead, on the table next to the chair, there was a wooden box full of what looked like small metal Frisbees, bigger than Jaffa Cakes but smaller than Digestives.

Oscar continued to look around the room as the little man fiddled with one of the drawers in his desk, mumbling something about a 'blasted' key. The walls were covered with framed photographs but it was hard to see them properly in the dim glow from the alphabet machine. Oscar squinted hard to try and get a better look. His eyes were just coming into focus when Mr Rouse asked him to take a seat. He was sure that the photograph he was looking at was Mr Rouse with some very serious army types with lots of medals and a few men in black suits with dark glasses, and what might have been rather large guns.

Mr Rouse asked if Oscar's mum wouldn't mind waiting in another room while he 'performed' the tests. He told her she could help herself to cake, which was enough to tempt her away.

"I'll just be in the other room, darling." she said, as she headed for the free cake. Oscar nodded like he didn't care but he wasn't so sure about being left alone with the strange little man.

Mr Rouse sat down and started to shuffle through

the papers on his desk. Oscar squinted at the letters trying to memorise them all.

"So, you've been having trouble with your vision?" he asked.

"Not really."

The little man held a moment's pause as if he knew Oscar was lying. His dad did a similar thing when he was checking if homework had been done, rooms tidied or sprouts eaten.

"Let's find out, shall we?"

Mr Rouse wheeled himself over to the screen on the wall in his chair and flicked a switch, making the letters even brighter.

"When you're ready, please start reading the letters from the top."

At first it was easy, but as Oscar got closer to the bottom the letters started to blur. He started to guess, watching Mr Rouse's expression as he did to try and get some sort of clue. But the old man's face gave nothing away.

"Looks a bit like a K but could be an R, maybe? No, it's definitely a… Beee?"

"Excellent, excellent," said Mr Rouse without even looking up.

The next twenty minutes were a bit of a blur. Mr Rouse fired random questions at him, mainly about solving crimes and detective work, which Oscar thought was strange as it had nothing to do with his eyesight, none of the questions even mentioned glasses. Mr Rouse tested his reflexes, hitting him on the knee and elbow with a small metal hammer, then more questions. Oscar hadn't even tried any glasses on; it felt more like an interrogation than an eye test.

Oscar watched and waited as the old man entered all of the test results into the computer on his desk. He was typing very quickly.

"Is everything OK?" checked Oscar, worried that maybe his eyes were that bad he was having to find out what was wrong with them on Google. Mr Rouse ignored his question and hit the enter key.

"Bravo!"

"Are my eyes OK?"

"Not exactly. You are quite shortsighted in your left eye, the right one not so much, but your test scores were most impressive, yes, most impressive."

Oscar was very confused.

"OK, let's try these." Mr Rouse picked up a pair of robot-looking glasses from the side. They were like the ones Oscar had seen on the Internet, the ones that looked like they might control your mind if you put them on as opposed to fix your eyesight. The old man's face was right next to Oscar's. He could tell that he had eaten something with onions in it for lunch and potentially some type of fish, followed by a mint to try and cover up the stink.

It hadn't worked.

Mr Rouse slipped the robot glasses on, picked up a couple of lenses and slid them into the slots on the glasses. Oscar noticed a red dot moving around the lettered screen. He waved his hand in front of the glasses and the red dot appeared on his hand. *I wonder what that's for?* he thought. If he had known it was a laser sight, the type used by government snipers and skilled assassins, he might have been a bit more careful.

Oscar was starting to like the idea of having glasses. He imagined having laser beam vision just like Superman, his favourite superhero. The old man turned to look at the screen and spotted the red dot whizzing about.

"Oh, I say!" he stammered whipping the glasses from Oscar's face, "Those are, erm … not for you."

Mr Rouse mumbled and grumbled away at himself for his mistake as he pulled out the next pair of glasses.

"Right, let's try these. What can you read now?" said the old man. Oscar started to read down the letters again and this time it was slightly easier. He managed to make it a couple of lines further down the board.

"Your father is a policeman, isn't he?" Mr Rouse asked as he tried another lens in front of Oscar's eyes.

"He's a detective actually," Oscar said proudly, not even thinking about how the strange optician would have known about his dad's job.

"I used to work with the boys in blue once upon a time," Mr Rouse said wheeling himself over to one of the photographs on the wall and pointing at the man stood next to him in the picture.

"This gentleman is a very dear friend of mine. One of the greatest detectives that ever lived."

Oscar got out of the chair and walked over to take a closer look at the photo.

"No way! That's Inspector Riley, isn't it?"

Mr Rouse nodded, "Of Scotland Yard, no less."

"He single-handedly caught 'The Purple Claw', didn't he?" exclaimed Oscar.

"Not quite!' Mr Rouse smiled, "He had a little help from his friends." Mr Rouse puffed his chest out and swaggered back to his desk. Oscar couldn't quite believe that the little man in front of him had played a part in taking down one of the most infamous thieves in the world, the first thief to have ever stolen the Crown Jewels.

"Can you keep a secret, my boy?"

Oscar did the Scout's honour salute so quickly that he nearly poked himself in the eye. Luckily, he still had the strange prototype glasses on so instead he just left a smudged fingerprint right in the middle of the lens.

"Yes, yes, of course," he said excitedly, "Scout's honour."

"Would you like to try some rather, erm, special glasses?" the old man whispered, "I think they will be the perfect fit."

"Are they like Elton John's?" Oscar whispered back. He didn't know why they were whispering.

"Why? What? Elton John?" The old man shook his head like a wet dog. "No, my young man, these aren't for pop music! They are top secret, classified, hi-tech, and if they fall into the wrong hands, they could be deadly!"

Oscar was struggling to wipe the smile off his face but he could see from the old man's reaction that he needed to look a little more serious.

"You can trust me!" Oscar said, in his deepest, gruffest voice.

Mr Rouse kept his eyes trained on the boy for one more minute before turning his back and walking over to the wall. He stood in front of a picture of a young lady who was wearing glasses. He was standing so close to it that Oscar thought he actually might kiss the photograph, that maybe it was Mr Rouse's sweetheart, but instead he removed his glasses and a beam of light came out of the picture and scanned the old man's face. It was an eye scanner to verify identity and as it verified Mr Rouse the strangest thing happened.

It wasn't the sound of the five or six locks securing the doors that seemed strange to Oscar, or the way that the wall the old man had been standing in front of started to move. He'd seen mystery doors in loads of films; you pull the book on the shelf and hey presto the secret door activates. No, what was strangest of all was the way all the other walls disappeared, like they were somehow invisible, but somehow still there.

"X-ray, one-way walls," said the old man, "I developed them myself."

Oscar looked around wide-eyed. He could see his mum in the next room flicking casually through one of the magazines in the waiting room. If he squinted he could see the photographs on the page she was reading of two famous-looking people on a beach and the words, 'BEACH BUMS'. That made him smile. He could see past her down through the endless sea of corridors. In the distance he thought he could make out people in a room full of screens, but they could have just as easily been anything, blurred out almost completely because of how far away they were.

"That is so cool!" Oscar squeaked.

"Yes, it is rather, isn't it? Absolutely pointless but great fun." beamed the old man. He typed into the watch on his wrist and a panel opened at the back of the room to reveal yet another room, "Come with me."

Oscar almost ran into him in his rush to get into the secret room. The walls in the smaller antechamber were covered in spectacles of all kinds, like an optical library or a real-life encyclopedia of glasses. There were glasses going right back to caveman times made out of what looked like bones and dinosaur teeth. There were knight's glasses with coats of arms, spaceman glasses, invisible glasses; they were particularly hard to see.

In the middle of the room, protected by a glass dome was a very normal-looking pair of glasses. They

27

were tortoiseshell, the same colour as Fred the cat from next door. The old man touched the glass dome and with a mechanical whir the case opened up. He carefully took the glasses out of the case and turned to face Oscar.

"Right," said Mr Rouse with a serious expression, "these are the glasses I think you should have. But be warned they are very powerful."

Oscar didn't hear him at first he was too busy looking around at the other glasses, specifically the ones that had mini rocket launchers fixed on either side. The old man followed his gaze.

"Oh, I see you like the old M16 specs. They are mainly for guerrilla warfare, not really for young boys."

"Monkeys wear glasses?" mused Oscar. Mr Rouse told him they weren't for that kind of gorilla.

Back in the seat the old man was busy measuring Oscar's face to make sure the new glasses fitted perfectly.

"Are you ready?" he asked.

Oscar nodded. The glasses slipped on and tucked comfortably behind his ears. The old man smiled.

"A perfect fit." Mr Rouse stepped out of the way. Oscar could see every detail of the room perfectly. He wasn't trying to see them, but he could even see the curly white hairs protruding out of the old man's nostrils. Even the tiniest letters at the bottom of the alphabet board were in perfect focus, but Oscar couldn't help but feel a bit disappointed. There were no missiles, no laser sights or computer read-out; he could just see.

Mr Rouse's smile was widening and becoming more mischievous.

"So, when you are ready, there is a button situated just behind your right ear. You may feel a cold sensation on the side of your head, but don't worry, they are just the neural probes aligning."

Probes? thought Oscar. He wasn't sure he wanted probes or probing for that matter. He pressed the button and the glasses whirred into life. He felt the cold sensation as the two probes attached just above either ear. At first, there was just a rumbling noise as the specs powered up, but then the lenses started to glow, filling with numbers, just like a computer he had once had; the one his father gave him from work, one with big buttons that clicked and the windy noise when you turned it on. Oscar had wanted a PlayStation but his dad said that this computer was much better, had more memory, apparently, and he would be able to write programs on it. Oscar had asked if he could play 'Killer Ninja' on it but it didn't look like he could.

The word 'mode' came up on the right lens.

"So, baby steps as they say," said the old man. Oscar's mind was already running away with itself.

Through the lenses of the spectacles the room and everything in it had transformed right in front of him into a real-life computer game. Even Mr Rouse was surrounded by a bright electronic outline. Oscar was so distracted he hardly noticed the word 'combat' flash up on the screen in red.

"This is awesome!" he said, passing his hands in front of his eyes and following the tracers they left in their wake.

"Should I worry about the flashing red thingy?" asked Oscar, "It seems to be getting faster?"

"Wait..." but before Mr Rouse could finish, Oscar's imagination had careered off into a world of combat. The laser beam that shot out of the glasses struck the alphabet screen on the wall, melting the letters off instantly.

"Quick! Think 'Stop'!" shouted the old man, as he hopped up and down like a small, agitated Leprechaun.

"Hey?!" said Oscar, as he looked to him for help, the beams tracking along as he moved his head, a smoking line in its wake. Mr Rouse dived under his desk just as the beams swept over his head, chopping the top of his lamp off.

"Think 'Stop'!"

Oscar closed his eyes tightly and thought *Stop!* as many times as he could. The laser stopped immediately and all that was left in the room was smoke and the smell of burning plastic. Mr Rouse brushed himself off as he struggled to clamber up from under the desk. Oscar jumped out of the seat to help the creaking old man.

"I'm really sorry about your lamp," Oscar said apologetically. "I'll buy you a new one."

"Oh my," said the old man looking around at the damage. "My fault. I should have probably explained the rules."

He gently removed the glasses from Oscar's face and using the buttons on the side switched the glasses to 'Safe' mode before handing them back.

"So, you have 'Combat' mode, which you seem to have got to grips with," explained the old man with a wink, "Then there's 'Search' mode and 'Night' mode too. 'Combat' mode is a last resort and should only be used if you are in grave danger. 'Search' mode will allow you to spot clues and decipher crimes and finally 'Night' mode is for when you are operating at night and you can't see."

He looked back at Oscar who still had his eyes shut tight in case he caused any more damage. He was unsure what to do; he didn't want to laser anything else.

"I think we need to work on your mind control before we switch off the safety." said Mr Rouse, pondering what might help Oscar regain his confidence.

"Mind control?" It sounded pretty sinister to Oscar.

"It's nothing to fear my boy. Why, Sherlock Holmes himself used to meditate to control his thoughts."

"He's just a character in a book though?"

"Well quite, but my point is all great detectives need to learn to control their minds. They must be crystal clear to find the clues that catch the crooks!"

It was almost turning into a speech.

"OK, but how do I do it? How do I learn?" asked Oscar, intrigued to find out more.

"I studied with Master Fung," continued the old man, "in the foothills of the Himalayas, but I don't suppose you can get time off school for a trip to Kathmandu?"

Oscar shook his head. "I don't think my mum would let me. I've only ever been to Majorca."

"Never mind, my boy. I don't doubt that you will master it over time. We will do it together. You will have a mind like a still pond by the time we have finished, but these things take time, and every detective must take time to learn his trade."

Oscar looked nervous, "I'm not really a detective though… and I don't really solve crimes."

Mr Rouse pulled his glasses down his nose and looked over the top of them at Oscar. "What do you want to be more than anything?"

"A detective…I guess," said Oscar doubtfully, "but I'm just a boy."

The old man raised a finger, seemingly struck by

an idea. He leant forward and rummaged around in his desk drawers pulling out an old, crinkled photograph, blowing a layer of dust off the top. The image was slightly faded by the sun, but you could just make out a young boy with spectacles on, standing proudly, shaking the hand of a policeman with lots of medals who was presenting him with his very own medal.

Oscar looked closer, "Is that you?"

"Yes, that's me. Just a boy like you, and I had just solved my first crime," he beamed, "The first one is always the toughest."

Chapter Four
The Cheese Phantom Strikes Again

As well as his 'Spectacular Spectacles,' Mr Rouse gave Oscar a normal pair of glasses to help stop the headaches and to make sure his newly found detective status wouldn't be blown in front of his mum.

He'd gone deep undercover.

Well, actually he hadn't. He had just stashed the 'Spectacular Spectacles' under his wardrobe in a tiny compartment at the bottom left-hand side where his dad dropped it on the floor the day they moved house. His dad had insisted on helping the removal men with the wardrobe but as he had shouted, "Left a bit! Left a bit!" he hadn't realised that the removal men he had partnered with misheard him and had interpreted it as "Lift! Lift!" The cupboard had fallen onto his dad's foot, cracking at the bottom and creating the perfect secret compartment. Oscar had hidden the glasses in there with the catapult his grandfather had given him, a bullet cartridge he had found in the woods and a small skull, of unknown origin, with theories ranging from mouse to dinosaur. The things that were kept in secret compartments were always important to young children. They were normally one of the first things they would show to any guest, along with tree houses, secret passages and dens. However, since putting the glasses in the compartment, Oscar hadn't gone near it. He was feeling the pressure the spectacles were having on him and thought he should confide in his mum. He had obviously been picked by Mr Rouse for a reason, he just didn't know it yet. He watched the new Superman film not long before he went to see Mr Rouse and there was a part where Superman was struggling with the pressure of being a superhero and saving the world and had gone and spoken to his mum. Oscar thought he should do the same. *If Superman can chat to his mum about saving the world then why can't I?*

"So Mum," Oscar started, thinking about the best way to phrase what he was going to say. "There is this boy and he has to solve crimes."

"Has he done his homework first?" his mum said without turning around from the ironing board. It was no good, he thought, she was way too clever to catch out. He decided not to say anything else and instead watched the Superman clip again.

He sat down in his dad's seat and searched for the clip. "It's not up to you to save the world." Superman's mum had said. Those words played over and over in his head.

Oscar thought about the scene long and hard as he tried to sleep that night. Before he had been given the glasses, all he had to worry about was tying his shoelaces, eating his greens and teaching Watson how to roll over. But everything had changed now.

That night he had a dream. He was in the park playing football and the ball had been hoofed into the back of the Morris's garden. Mr Morris was getting a bit cheesed off with people playing football next to his house and you would often catch him spying through the holes in the back of his fence left by the many misplaced penalty kicks, waiting to catch the perpetrator.

One of the older boys from the park had told Oscar and his friends that Mr Morris had built a series of traps to catch the kids who kicked the balls against his fence. They sounded a bit like the ones in Indiana Jones; the final one being a large rock in the shape of a football that rolled down the garden if the tripwire was sprung, crushing everything in its path. The boys didn't really believe the rumours but had still moved slightly further away from the house. In the dream, Trevor 'The Hoof' Harries still managed to kick the ball over the fence into Morris's garden. As he ran from the scene of the crime, disappearing from the park, he shouted over his shoulder that Oscar was goalie so he would have to be the one to collect the ball.

Oscar really didn't want to be pulverised by the rock trap but he had only just been given the ball and it was a Euro 2016 special; he wanted it back.

Suddenly, there was a flash of red and blue and Superman landed on the penalty spot. He was smaller in real life and it looked like he hadn't shaved for a while. His suit seemed a little too tight and scuffed in places, he even had some ketchup down his top.

Oscar was a bit worried about him. This wasn't what he thought Superman looked like; he was a 'Man of Steel' not a man who spilt food on his top. He was supposed to be flash, smart, well dressed and definitely clean. He looked a little bit tired and fed up.

After they retrieved the ball (Superman did it in the end; flew over the fence, picked it up and flew back) Oscar asked Superman if he wanted to come back and have some squash. Superman said he would be delighted to join him and they sat in the back garden drinking orange squash on the swings.

"Are you sure you're OK?" Oscar asked, worried about his new superhero friend.

"It's all got a bit too much to be honest," said the caped wonder.

"You probably just need a break. My nan has a villa in Majorca. I'm sure you could stay there. A break is as good as a holiday, she says."

"Crime never takes a break, my friend. Evil has no holidays!"

He was very dramatic. At this point, he stood up and put his hands on his hips; he did that a lot. He turned theatrically, his cape swooshing round with him.

"I need your help Oscar." he said pointing at the boy.

As Superman spoke the words they started to merge together, then more voices joined in until there were lots of people shouting for help.

Oscar sat bolt upright in bed. That was it; he was going to solve crimes. He was going to help save the world! He jumped out of bed and put his hands on his hips hoping that would be the first step. Saving the world was a big job, though, so he thought it would be best to cut his teeth on something a bit smaller; work out how to use his new glasses whilst setting up a local crime bureau. He looked up the word 'bureau'. It was a good word for office he thought. *If it's good enough for the FBI it's good enough for me.* He decided to deputise Watson and his best friend, Jude, who on hearing about his new role had immediately started saluting. In fact, he saluted so much Oscar had to tell him to stop.

Jude might have only been six but he was not only Oscar's best friend, he was also his most resourceful. He always had the bits and bobs you needed: string, marbles, a smile, unusual snacks.

Jude's mum was useful too; she made cakes for the local cake shop. Oscar thought cake would be the perfect temptation to lure people to come and pay a visit to their new bureau desk, which was basically the old kitchen table he'd taken out of the shed with a piece of card taped to the front that had 'WE ARE DETECTIVES' written on it.

Oscar also put a sign on Watson's bed, which read 'DOG-TECTIVE', but Watson had eaten most of it by 10am and now it just said 'DOG.' Jude wrote 'Cake' in red paint on another piece of cardboard, but he had written the C of cake backwards and the red paint had spilt down the card making it look a bit like blood.

"Is that blood?" asked the twins from number thirty-nine, both pointing at the sign.

"Might be!" Oscar replied, joking around. The twins froze for a moment, turned to look at each other in shock, then stared between the dripping paint and Oscar before running off screaming. They did everything together; it was a bit annoying.

That cut short the first day on the job as Oscar spent most of it apologising to the twins' mum and was then sent to bed.

On the second day of being detectives, they ran out of cake and no one seemed that interested without snacks. It was Millionaire Shortbread, one of Oscar's favourites; squidgy caramel, crunchy biscuit base. Jude had shown him how to stick three pieces together, squish them up and shove them all in his mouth at the same time, which they had then tried several times with great success, hence the empty cake plate. Oscar decided to retire to the kitchen and sulk. Jude went home because he felt sick.

"I'm giving up on crime fighting!" he said to his mum as he banged around trying to find his favourite cup.

"That's a shame." she said turning to look at the slumped, soon to be retired crime fighter.

"I can't even find my favourite cup!"

"Come on, sit down and tell me what's wrong."

"People don't care about crime, they just care about cake."

"You like cake too."

Oscar did like cake but all he could think about were all the criminals running around whilst he sat there with his mum. Then he couldn't help but burp as he thought a bit more about cake.

Damn you cake and all your nice bits! he thought.

"I just need one crime, that's all!" he growled as he pushed his chair back and stomped off up the stairs to his room. He slammed the door so hard that Watson let out a fearful howl. It wasn't long before he heard his mum's footsteps coming up the stairs. He dived into bed and pulled the cover over his head, assuming he was in trouble for the door slamming. It was still light under the duvet cover so he could make out the outline of his mum coming through the door before he felt her sit down on the end of the bed. Oscar waited with baited breath.

"No need to get cross. I think you are a brilliant detective."

"I can't be a detective if I don't have any crimes to solve!"

His mum pulled down the duvet. Oscar pulled it back up.

"I think I might have a crime for you to solve." she said, pulling the duvet back down again.

"No you haven't…have you?"

"It's a very serious crime and it could be dangerous. Someone has stolen our cheese."

Oscar sighed a heavy sigh, "That doesn't sound like a serious crime to me. Thanks for trying though mum."

"So tell me who took it? Didn't you ever hear of 'The Case of the Missing Brie'?" she asked.

Oscar sat up in bed and reached over to the bedside table where he kept his notepad on which he had written, 'We Are Detectives' in bubble letters. He had given one to Jude too, when he deputised him, as a welcome gift from the bureau.

It was meant for general crime stuff and to write reports if they saw anything peculiar. He licked the tip of his pen, he had seen a policeman do it in an old film. He hadn't realised it was a pencil in the film and now the pen had left a funny taste in his mouth and a blue spot. He held the pen paused over the page, his mum watched in anticipation. Oscar wasn't sure what to write.

"OK I suppose I can try and investigate it then. First question, what's Brie?"

"A type of cheese."

Oscar scribbled down the word 'cheese'. "Is it a rare or expensive kind of cheese?"

"Very!"

"And when did said rare cheese go missing?"

His mum started to pace back and forth to make it all a bit more serious.

"So, it was last Wednesday. I arrived at the supermarket at 0800 hours. Usually I go down the fruit and veg aisle first but an announcement about a biscuit offer made me go straight to the biscuit aisle to pick up some of those cookies you like."

"The ones with the gooey centre?" Oscar verified.

"Affirmative."

Oscar was enjoying his mum's detective style speak.

"As I approached the cookies, I passed the crackers and I thought, '*Ooh, I have some nice Brie in the fridge,*' so I went and got myself some of those little crackers I love, you know with the cheesy little bits in?"

"The nutty ones?"

"Roger that."

Oscar wrote down the word 'crackers' and 'nuts'. He still couldn't work out if she was being serious or not so he wrote 'Is mum…' in front of both of the words and added numerous question marks.

"Well, the next day, around 11am, I made myself a little cup of tea, went to the fridge and the Brie had just disappeared."

"Things don't just disappear? You and dad do eat a lot of cheese. Maybe you just ate it? It's not a crime to eat your own cheese." he continued as he closed his book.

"We do love cheese, that's true. But I know it wasn't me and your father said he hadn't touched it… so who did it?"

Watson put a paw over his eyes; he was always the go-to guy if there were any missing food mysteries to solve, and besides, he wasn't a fan of French cheese, he only really liked Cheddar or Double Gloucester.

"Oh well, never mind. I just thought it was maybe something to investigate, but if you think cheese can just disappear maybe it's not?" baited his mother as she sauntered out of the room.

Oscar phoned Jude to see if he thought it was a crime worth investigating. He said they should immediately draw a line around where the cheese had last been spotted, like they did with dead bodies at the scene of a crime. Oscar wasn't sure if his mum would like them drawing all over the fridge, but admired his friend's thinking.

"I'd better come over!" said Jude, "Forthwith!" he added. That was another thing Jude did quite a lot, he came out with the most astonishingly clever words.

Five minutes later there was a knock at the door. Even though Jude only lived two doors down he had ridden his bike over so he could show Oscar his latest customisation. Oscar opened the door and there was Jude, saluting.

Jude had wrapped paper around the whole frame of his bike, drawn sirens on the back of his seat and written the word 'Police' everywhere, but the touch he was most proud of was the drawing of him, Oscar and Watson, catching a rather dubious character in a stripy jumper and a mask that he had expertly drawn on his number plate that hung on his handlebars.

"That's us," said Jude, tracing his finger across the drawing as Oscar bent down to look at the artwork more closely.

"Good work, little buddy," said Oscar. He spotted that Jude was growling a bit so he rephrased it. "Good work, big buddy?" Jude stopped growling.

The two of them stood in front of the fridge taking notes as Watson sniffed around. Jude looked over Oscar's shoulder and mimicked him as best he could. He wrote cheese a couple of times, then gave up and drew a picture of his bike.

"Hello Jude," said Oscar's mum, "I've just seen your bike outside, nice work," she smiled, passing him to open the fridge. In a flash Jude dived in front of her, spreading himself out as wide as he could, blocking off access to the fridge door.

"Sorry Mrs Chesterton, I can't let you do that," said Jude, as politely as he could.

"He's right, Mum. Good work Jude."

Jude saluted.

"It is?" said Oscar's mum confused.

"That fridge is an official crime scene!"

"It's also my fridge and I need to start making your dinner."

"What are you making?" enquired Oscar. With one hand, the other one still guarding the fridge door, Jude pulled his notepad out of his inside pocket and flipped it open.

"Spaghetti," said Oscar's mum.

Jude wrote down the word 'Pasta' because it was a bit shorter and he couldn't think if it was a 'G' or a 'K' in spaghetti. The boys now had a tough decision to make. This was their favourite dish, but the security of the crime scene was at stake. They looked at each other and shrugged, the thought of spaghetti overruling the need to keep the fridge closed off.

"OK, you can enter the fridge," replied Oscar, "but make no mistake, we are watching you."

"Noted."

After dinner, Oscar asked if Jude could have a sleepover. They had decided to try to lay a trap for the cheese thief that very night. Jude's mum said he could but he would have to go home and get his pyjamas and a toothbrush. Whilst his friend popped home, Oscar thought long and hard about getting the 'Spectacular Spectacles' out. If he was going to solve a crime surely this was the best time to put them to use? He had looked up mind control on the Internet, remembering that this was the thing Mr Rouse had told him he needed to master. His first search results were quite scary with images of Zombie-like people with blank eyes stumbling around, but then he stumbled across something called 'meditation' and images of wise old men with white hair sitting on misty mountains. It seemed simple to Oscar, just sitting still with your eyes closed, hands on your knees, thumb and forefinger pressed together. He sat down on the floor, crossed his legs and closed his eyes, expecting to find immediate peace. Instead of a calm pond or a quiet mind there were a million thoughts whizzing around like rockets. He opened his eyes. *Perhaps I should practice a bit more?* He made a note in his detective journal to speak to Mr Rouse about it the next time he saw him.

Whilst Oscar struggled with mind control, Jude was at home buried deep in his fancy dress box, throwing clothes all over his room. He eventually settled on his Gruffalo onesie in case things got violent, then he could terrorise the cheese phantom with his Gruffalo face. He showed it to Oscar and Watson and they all agreed it was frightening; Watson even whined.

"Night boys," called Oscar's mum up the stairs.

"Lights out in twenty minutes," added his dad.

"OK!" both the boys replied in unison.

They lay in bed waiting, listening to the house wind itself down. The click of the kettle being put on for the last cup of tea before bed, the sound of the back door being locked, the lounge door closing, the latch on the front door being switched, the creak of the first stair, the cord of the bathroom light being pulled, the whir of toothbrushes.

Jude was busy practising his Gruffalo growl, *silent but deadly*, he thought. Oscar had decided against telling Jude about the glasses straight away, as sometimes he got a bit upset if he didn't have the same things as Oscar and besides, he didn't want to blow the house up or destroy the fridge with any stray laser beams.

When they were sure his parents were asleep, they tiptoed down to the first landing. Watson tiptoed after them.

"Wait!" whispered Jude, grabbing his friend's arm.

"What is it?"

Jude pointed to the shadow they were making on the wall. He raised his arms in a 'scary creature' type way.

"Scary?"

Oscar assured him it was terrifying and had made his blood run cold, but told Jude to save it for when they came face to face with the 'Cheese Phantom'. They had come up with several names: Cheese Fiend, The Great Cheesendo, and Cheddar Claws (a late entry from Jude) before settling on the Cheese Phantom.

"You wait here and keep look out," Oscar instructed, before carefully opening the back door that led to the garage. Jude told Watson to keep a look out and followed his friend. Watson looked on curiously and listened. After a few moments of banging around, the boys returned to the kitchen. Oscar had seen a movie where they used fishing line as a tripwire between the windows to alert the detective when the bad guys tried to break in. In the film they had tied a bell to the fishing wire as a makeshift alarm.

Oscar didn't have a bell but Jude improvised and tied the fishing wire between the back door and the conservatory door with a saucepan to act as a makeshift alarm. Once the trap was set, they crept back upstairs, left the bedroom door slightly ajar and then hopped back into bed. Within minutes, they both fell asleep and Oscar started to dream.

In the dream he was in the skate park, sitting at the top of the ramp contemplating if this was going to be the day he was finally going to drop in. He had set his board up on the rim of the ramp, wobbling as he readied himself for the big moment. Suddenly, the same flash of red and blue he had seen in the park caught his eye and there was Superman standing in front of him. It turned out that the man of steel was very grateful that Oscar had taken the time to talk to him the previous day and, in return, had made some delicious egg and cress sandwiches for them both to share.

"Wow, these are really nice. Thanks, Superman."

"My friends call me Kal-El," said Superman, "Son of Jor-El."

"My friends call me Oscar," replied Oscar, "Son of Matthew."

"Pleased to meet you again, son of Matthew."

They discussed the trials and tribulations of saving the world again. Oscar told him that he thought people were more interested in cake than justice. Superman agreed it was a close call. He said, "With great cake comes great responsibility."

Oscar didn't really understand but he nodded anyway. He was distracted; a strange noise had started up and it was whirling around his head.

"Can you hear that noise?"

Superman shook his head. It sounded a bit like a saucepan banging against a tiled floor.

That is exactly what it is, thought Oscar, waking suddenly from his dream. He sat bolt upright, as did Watson. Jude continued to snore.

Oscar could hear a strange sort of groaning mixed with the clattering of the saucepan coming from downstairs.

"To the kitchen, Watson! Our trap has been sprung!"

Watson looked over at the sleeping Jude.

"Jude, wake up!" whispered Oscar, as Watson set about licking the boy's face. Jude sat up, saluting before jumping out of bed and adopting his Gruffalo stance.

Oscar thought about putting on the 'Spectacular Spectacles,' but they were still hidden under the cupboard and there was no time to waste. He grabbed his torch and the intrepid threesome crept down the stairs. The noise was indeed coming from the kitchen and a dim light was coming from under the door.

Oscar waved his hand back and forth by the side of his head. He had seen an army person do it in a film, but no one understood what the signal meant; they were all frozen in terror thinking about what the Cheese Phantom might look like.

"Will he actually be made of cheese?" whispered Jude as he tried to maintain his growl. Oscar was about to answer when his mum walked slowly past them, half asleep, straight into the kitchen. Watson started to bark thinking that the Cheese Phantom might think that Mum was a cracker.

"Charge!" yelled Jude as he stormed the kitchen.

Now everybody was in the kitchen, including Oscar's dad, who was on the floor with a saucepan on his head, a rather angry look on his face and what looked suspiciously like a squashed piece of cheese in his hand. Oscar and the Detective Bureau, aka Jude and Watson, had solved their first crime, and 'The Case of the Cheese Phantom' was closed. Mum told everyone to go to bed and, with a less than amused face, told Dad he was back on his special 'cottage cheese' diet.

Chapter Five
The Big Boned Fella

Oscar hadn't put his 'Spectacular Spectacles' on for days, after he tried toasting some bread with the laser sights and ended up setting it on fire, creating a black cloud of smoke that filled the whole kitchen and set the smoke alarm off. *I can control my mind!* he thought, and closed his eyes trying to calm himself down. He would try meditating for a few more days and then put them back on, outside, in a field, away from anyone, miles away from any toast.

To distract himself from the glasses dilemma Oscar had been keeping himself busy with preparations for his school's Sports Day. He had been getting up early and jogging to the park, and then, using two old Coke cans he set up a start and finishing line. He had been picked to run in both the two hundred metres and the four hundred metre relay.

He hadn't been the first choice for either race in previous years but due to a particularly nasty outbreak of chickenpox, a few of the regular speed demons had dropped out. He was doing quite well with his training. He had borrowed his dad's digital watch and managed to shave thirty seconds off his personal best.

Sports Day was never normally an event filled with surprises. The usual people ran and won the usual races and everyone else filled in the gaps. The weather had been hot and the ground was dry and desert like, solid as a rock. Patches of grass had worn away and the park and the school fields had turned a shade of yellow. It wouldn't have looked out of place if the odd flock of gazelles or pride of lions had been spotted prowling across the scorched ground. It was so dry that Mr Robinson, from number forty-two, had resorted to watering his garden at night to avoid the hosepipe ban. He thought no one was watching, but one night as the sun dropped down behind the chimney tops Oscar popped the spectacles on to see if 'Night Mode' worked. He could see all sorts of things going on: frogs hopping out of ponds, foxes scavenging through bins and people who should have been in bed, lurking around in the shadows.

There were two days to go before the big day and the chickenpox plague reached epidemic levels. For once, the kids at school were talking about who might win the races. The only race that wasn't really raising any eyebrows was the hundred metres. Three of the favourite athletes were still in the running, but there was an outsider who had made the cut: Rupert Walker. This was a mystery in itself.

It wouldn't be accurate to say Rupert was big for his age; in fact, he was a modern-day giant, a human

Goliath. Some kids joked that if you put money in him you could get chocolate bars out. Oscar didn't join in on those jokes as he thought it was a bit mean and clearly not true. His mum told him he was just 'big boned'. Oscar's nan said the same thing about Rupert; he's just big boned and it isn't nice to call him fat. Oscar agreed and came up with his own nickname, 'The Big Fella'.

Oscar had bumped into Rupert on several of his morning trips to the park with Watson. Rupert was running alongside his dad who was riding next to him on an electric bicycle with a big stopwatch hanging around his neck. Rupert was really trying to be a serious contender, and Oscar admired that, but no one else held out much hope for him against the other runners, one of whom was already taking part in county races against boys twice his age and wore those special tight running shorts that you see athletes wearing on TV.

It was a matter of days before Sports Day and Oscar upped his regime to three raw eggs in the morning (a diet he had seen in a film about a boxer). *No pain no gain!* he thought as he held his nose and swallowed his third yolk.

The weather hadn't let up and the desert like conditions continued. Each day Mr Hudson, the PE teacher, and his eager teaching assistants stood in the middle of the field tapping the ground with their feet and tutting. Occasionally they looked at the sky as if praying to the weather gods. The weather had been so hot that they weren't even allowed to turn the sprinklers on. Local council posters had now been stuck up everywhere reminding the locals that there was a hosepipe ban in place until further notice. Mr Robinson had tried to remove most of them.

The school field was off limits the day before the main event. Mr Benson the caretaker, pipe in mouth, paced seriously around the field with the paint machine, tracing over all the lines for the running lanes. He even got creative, using pieces of card with numbers cut out as stencils to mark the lanes.

The smaller running tracks were all inside the larger track, which Mr Benson had left until last to paint. Last year he had ended up leaving white footprints on his wife's new carpet in the conservatory and had to spend the night sleeping on the sofa.

Chapter Six
The Moonwalk

Oscar woke early, covered in sweat. He had closed his window because the foxes had been chatting outside which always made Watson whine in his sleep. He stretched as he stepped out of his bed and scratched his side like a monkey.

He felt the radiator thinking maybe Mum had left the heating on, but it was stone cold. Watson slowly rose from his bed, shaking himself off, his tongue hanging from the side of his mouth in an attempt to cool himself down.

"Are you awake?" shouted his mum up the stairs. Oscar was already up. In fact, he was half way through his first set of warm-up stretches he had found online. He planned to follow his warm-up with five minutes of meditation, which he was getting much better at. He could now stop almost all of his thoughts, except for one, *'Can I win?'*

The latest fitness video he downloaded had four main stretches. The first one was a lunge, the second involved pinning alternate legs up to his bum, the third a sort of weird, bendy leg thing that made him look like the stick insect he once owned called

Twiggy. The final stretch involved him reaching up to the ceiling and then lowering his fingers down to his toes.

All of his bouncing around had started the light swinging in the kitchen.

"Will you please stop jumping around up there!" called Mum.

Oscar insisted on variety when it came to his nutritious breakfast regime in the build-up to Sports Day. He had upgraded from eggs and found a recipe for an egg and banana shake and settled on that for the final push. He had got increasingly bored of just eggs, but it was the last day before he could go back to slurping the chocolatey milk at the end of a bowl of his favourite cereal: Coco Pops.

"How are you feeling about the big race?" his mum asked over her shoulder.

"It's cool," he gurgled, as he forced down the rest of his shake.

"I'm not sure it will be, it's going to be very hot today, so you'll have to make sure you wear some sunscreen."

Oscar considered explaining the difference between 'cool' as in it will all be good and 'cool' as in the opposite of hot, but decided that it might just go straight over her head.

"Is Dad coming?" Oscar asked doubtfully. He kind of knew that the answer would be no, his dad was always working and had only managed to ever make it to one of Oscar's Sports Days but, even then, he had been on the phone most of the time. He didn't hate his dad for his lack of attendance, he just wanted him there, but he understood that it took a lot of effort to become a good detective.

It took commitment and time. Oscar was dedicated too; he had spent four hours on Saturday re-watching the 'Adventures of Sherlock Holmes' box set.

"You have to work hard to get the things you want," Oscar's nan always said.

On the morning of Sports Day, Oscar and his mum had to leave early because the parking spaces on the green outside of school got pretty packed. The order of the Sports Day races was always the same. First, of all the juniors had their races: egg and spoon, the sack race and the grand finale, the three-legged race. The egg and spoon had been known to get messy. One year it had actually been cancelled because of Edward, who, after the incident, became known as 'Eggward'.

It was two years ago and the fever of Sports Day had gripped the school more than ever before. The Head Teacher had decided to make the children paint the eggs with the face of the prince and princess who were getting married. The mini competitors were all lined up ready to go when Mr Benson had come out of the sports hall, a confused look on his face and an empty set of egg crates in his hand.

The eggs had been stolen.

Eventually, following the painted, glittering eggshell trail, they found Edward asleep under a tree at the top of the school field.

They didn't know if they should punish Edward or write to the Guinness Book of Records. He had eaten every single egg, surely it had to be some sort of record? *Criminals always leave a clue*, Oscar thought. *The perfect crime simply doesn't exist.* Today the eggs weren't painted, no princes or princesses were getting married, but the flags were still flying and the crowds were massing.

The competitors were encouraged to watch all the races and support their other team members. A few of the mums had brought umbrellas with them because the weather report that day had said the heat would pick up by mid-afternoon and the sun would be very big, or at least, that's how it looked on the TV. The map of Britain that the weather lady stood in front of was literally covered in giant yellow blazing suns, as if they were multiplying before your very eyes and would soon cover the whole country.

Oscar was a little bit bored. He liked watching the other races but there was so much faffing around in between. He decided to take a walk with Watson. Dogs were allowed to attend Sports Day if they were kept on a lead. Watson hated his lead and often tried to shake it off. He was perfectly in control of himself, he thought, unless he:

a. smelt food

b. saw a cat

c. got an itch on his privates

d. had his tummy tickled

Oscar had spoken to him about it before they left the house and had even given him a bit of cheese to soften the blow, but still it irked the little dog.

Oscar thought he would do a little lap around the field. He liked people watching and he had found a new function on his spectacles that slowed down time. Not literally: it recorded what was happening and then instantly played it back in slow motion. Mr Rouse had told him it was so that he could accurately observe a crime scene and slow things right down so he could pick out what everyone was doing and spot the clues a bit more easily. It was a bit like having a video recorder in your head. Oscar had often sat and thought of times when it would be useful to slow down things in real life, like the time he pulled the handbrake off in his dad's car and it rolled down the hill outside school and smashed into a lamppost. Or maybe in maths exams where they had to do lots of fractions and he got in a right muddle. He had found the perfect use for the 'Slow Mo' mode; he stared at the over-excited crowd of keen parents and then slowed them right down. The crowd looked a bit nuts; mouths slowly opening and closing, arms waggling around. Oscar went and stood by the finishing line and watched the runners raise their arms as they crossed over the line. *People look very funny when they are winning,* he thought.

He was so busy playing around with his spectacles that he had strayed into the middle of the field where the fabled hundred metre track was. He felt a hand on his shoulder and turned around to see the disgruntled face of Mr Benson.

"I'm afraid you're not allowed on this part of the field young man. You know that," he said, crossing his arms and nodding over at the 'Keep Off The Grass' sign. Oscar took a moment to realise where he was. This took a bit longer than it should have done because he had accidently left the 'Slow-Motion' switched on.

"Sorry, Mr Benson. I didn't realise where I was," Oscar said as he looked up and down the one hundred metre track.

"I must say you have done a good job with the grass. It looks much, erm, shinier than the rest of the field."

Mr Benson didn't want to react but Oscar could see that his compliment had made its way through. If they had both looked a little bit closer, they would have realised something wasn't quite right, but Mr Benson was too busy being smug and moving Oscar and Watson on.

Oscar thought he should go and try and find his mum again so he could leave Watson with her as his race was coming up soon. On his way, he ran into Rupert. They did occasionally speak to each other as they had gone to under-fives football together on the recreational ground.

"Hey Rupert."

Rupert tried to turn to see who it was but he was right in the middle of an elaborate stretching routine whilst trying to drink some sort of funny energy milkshake.

"Hey Oscar," he eventually managed as he tugged his legs out of the splits position. It looked as though the shiny, tight-fitted running suit was about to give way and, suddenly, Rupert would just be standing there in his pants.

"Good luck with the race today," said Oscar.

He thought Rupert must have been feeling nervous as he had never been in a race on Sports Day before. Rupert could only manage a weak smile; he was dreading the race. For the last few nights he had suffered from awful nightmares about falling over and everyone laughing at him, or not even really getting over the starting line before all the other boys finished. Oscar could see he was nervous but wasn't sure what to say; he was feeling the same way.

He dropped Watson off with his mother who wished him luck. Watson gave him a motivational woof send off. He would have dabbed but he was a dog and he would have fallen over.

Oscar liked the beginning of races, all the runners standing in line shaking their legs and arms waiting for the call.

"On your marks!"

The boys crouched down. Oscar looked up and down the line at the other runners. Now it was time to see if all those raw eggs really worked, if all the eggy farts he kept getting into trouble for were worth it. He had watched Usain Bolt at least a hundred times on YouTube. He'd watched him focus on the finishing line, never looking back, and keeping his knees up really high. For a split second, Oscar wondered what was going through the heads of the other runners as they looked ahead at the track. *You've got this*, he thought.

Everything closed in on Oscar. He visualised his legs pumping up and down, his arms slicing through the air. He thought of the spectacles and what a great detective he would become if he mastered them. *Life is so exciting I can taste it!* he thought, but then he realised it was just the eggs. All those thoughts faded as the starting gun raised and the shot rang out around the field. It was so loud it made Watson bark and Oscar's mum jump.

The race was on. Oscar knew that he had to get into a good position before they hit the first bend because after that all the runners would fall into line and if you got stuck in the pack it would be hard to break free. Oscar pictured the finishing line and bursting through it. As they crossed the line for the first time, Oscar was in fourth place, but his legs still felt good and he could taste something he thought might be victory. It might also have been the tail end of the burp he did at the start of the race.

The heat seemed to be picking up along with the fever of the crowd as they anticipated the end of the race. Oscar was hot on the heels of the boy in first place now. He'd never expected to be there, but there he was.

He could win. Victory was within his grasp.

The rest of the pack started to trail and Oscar could feel the space between him and the rest of the runners opening up. For a moment, everything slowed as the boy in front momentarily turned to see how far he was out in front. Oscar put his head down seeing his chance for victory.

He thought of watching Watson running in the fields near his house, so happy he was almost smiling, he could hear his pal's barks of encouragement somewhere in the distance. He stretched his legs out and started to dip his body down. He had read that was the way to win: stick your neck right out and hope you don't fall flat on your face.

With the finish line in sight, Oscar closed his eyes and when he opened them again he looked around at the crowd jumping up and down: he had won! Across the other side of the field, he could see his mum jumping up and down with Watson. The other runners came up and shook his hand as he looked across at Jude running towards him, his mouth open and his arms waving in the air. The two friends prepared to jump around together. Oscar had put Jude in charge of celebrations, a job he had taken very seriously.

The previous day Jude had asked his mum if she could help him research celebrations and had come up with a shortlist: the backflip, dab, the moonwalk, the samba, the finger snap. He had hurt his finger trying to snap them together so he settled on an invention of his own, 'The Moon Dab', a combination of two of his favourites and a move that they could do together. They were only halfway through the moonwalk bit when Mr Benson stepped in and moved them on. Jude continued to dab as they were ushered to the sidelines to make way for the one hundred metres, the main event.

Chapter Seven
Slippery When Wet

Oscar and Jude dabbed continuously for at least fifteen minutes. They had even convinced Oscar's mum to have a go; it almost started a Mexican dab as a few of the other parents joined in.

The runners were taking their place on the hundred metre starting line. Mr Benson was trying to get Rupert's dad off the track, he was barking some last-minute words of motivation at Rupert. Mr Hudson stepped up to the line and raised his starting gun.

"On your marks!" he shouted, and the boys lowered into their starting positions.

"Get set!"

The line raised back up ready to go and a low, murmuring chuckle moved across the crowd as a few people noticed Rupert was picking his nose. He did that when he was nervous.

Mr Hudson fired the starting gun and the runners were off. In fairness to Rupert, he started well and wasn't too far off the pace when everything started to get a little bit weird.

The boy out in the lead from the red team was the first to go; out of nowhere he started to stagger before flying head over heels onto the grass. Shortly after, the boy from the blue team did exactly the same, quickly followed by the green team runner. As the three runners slipped around trying to get back on their feet, Rupert steadily kept up his pace and, without any of the other runners it was Rupert's race to win.

The crowd watched in astonishment, mouths wide open as he sailed across the line and promptly returned to picking his nose. It was an image that would stay in Oscar's head for the next few days. He obviously had a really big bogey up there.

The hush of the crowd was soon replaced by the whole of the yellow team erupting into applause as they realised that Rupert's win meant that they had snatched the Sports Day victory from the red team by one solitary point.

"Rupert, Rupert give us a wave!" came the cry from the crowd. He even got a kiss from the head girl, Suzy Havers.

The crowd dispersed after the medals had all been handed out. Rupert's dad promptly took the medal off his son and bustled him off to the car. Oscar watched closely, his eyes tracking back to the hundred-metre track. He was pleased for Rupert, he deserved the applause but there was something suspicious about the whole affair.

At dinner that night, Oscar asked his mum if she thought there was anything peculiar about Rupert winning the race. She said it was a mysterious victory but that it was just one of those things.

Oscar decided it was time to call in Mr Rouse and ask him what he thought, but before he did that, he thought it was best to come up with a name for the investigation. He had borrowed some of the brown folders his dad used for his cases at work. He had used one for 'The Cheese Phantom' and stored it under the cupboard where he kept the spectacular spectacles after he had written 'closed' on the front with a big red marker.

After dinner he popped upstairs, grabbed his specs from the hiding place and headed out to the shed where he had decided to set up HQ. He nailed the 'We Are Detectives' sign over the door and moved all of the garden equipment into the garage to make room for the beanbags he had taken from the lounge and the old art easel his mum had been given for Christmas a few years back but had never used. It was perfect for an 'incident' board. A board where you stick all the clues, and string and pins.

"Right Watson, we need to come up with a name for our first big case, well, second case if we include 'The Cheese Phantom,' but that was my dad so it doesn't really count."

Watson barked in agreement. Oscar had looked on the Internet and found out that the process of coming up with ideas was often referred to as 'brainstorming'. It sounded quite painful but it seemed it was just a case of thinking a lot. He decided to write down some words to get started: sports day, big fella, shock win, tight Lycra and big bogey. In brainstorming he'd heard that no idea was a bad idea. He wasn't sure that was true – once, Jude had eaten a whole packet of extra strong mints and his face had turned blue. The world was full of bad ideas.

He stepped back from the board and closed his eyes hoping that when he opened them the answer would be there. But, alas, it was not. He slumped down onto the beanbag.

"Who am I kidding, Watson? If I can't even come up with a name for the case, how am I supposed to solve a real mystery?" moaned Oscar. He took the spectacles off and threw them on the floor next to him. Watson shook himself off, walked over to where Oscar was sitting, picked the glasses up gently in his mouth and waggled them at him.

Oscar looked down at his dog.

"You may as well have them, Watson."

But Watson wasn't going to let him give up and he gently dropped them into Oscar's lap.

"OK Watson, maybe you're right. I should try again with these on. Let's see if they help."

He slipped the glasses onto his head and pressed the 'On' button by his left ear. The glasses came to life; the cursor in the right-hand lens flashed, waiting for him to think up a command. *Problem solving,* thought Oscar. The mode button flashed and a second later the words 'What is the problem?' appeared on the lenses.

"Right spectacles, I need a name for our new case."

Oscar hauled himself up and walked over to the board where he had written the words from the brainstorm. As he stared at the words on the board in front of him, they started to move around as if the glasses were re-ordering them or searching for other words that matched, like when you see the arrivals board at an airport flick through to reveal the latest flights to land.

"They're doing it, Watson!" he shouted triumphantly, and one by one letters slotted into place to form new words on the lenses in front of him. He kept thinking about the race hoping it would help them create. He thought about watching Rupert's training, how the sun had got stronger and stronger that day, how it didn't make sense that the grass would have been wet. So why did the other boys slip over? As the thoughts flew through his mind the words finally formed and flashed up on the right hand lens. 'The Mystery Victory'.

Chapter Eight
The Investigation Begins

The next day, Oscar was up early again. He was going to go to the library to try and find some books on solving crimes. He packed his bag with his detective folder and told his mum he would be back for lunch. He was just about to leave when he realised he had forgotten his spectacles. He ran upstairs, grabbed them off the side and stopped in front of the hallway mirror. He slipped the glasses on and for a moment remembered how much he had hated the thought that he might have to start wearing glasses. A big smile spread across his face. *Glasses are kind of cool*, he thought, winking at himself before darting out of the door.

It was the weekend and with the tropical weather showing no sign of let up the library was empty. Most people headed to the beach, the local pool or just stayed in the garden enjoying the sun. The day had a real holiday feel to it; car windows down with songs blurting out into the sunshine, the smell of sunscreen wafting around.

Oscar asked the lady at the reception desk if they

had any books about crime solving.

"What sort of crime?" she asked, as she flicked through the pages on the screen in front of her. "Usually I get asked if I have any books on gardening," she continued tapping away vigorously.

"Murder?" she asked, looking him up and down suspiciously. Oscar thought quickly he didn't want to become a suspect.

"I'm joking!" She was finding herself a lot funnier than Oscar was, so he did a fake laugh to keep her happy.

"Good one."

She was still laughing, the noise reminded Oscar a bit of the Siamese cats that sat on the garage roof opposite his house.

"No murders here, just a homework project." he said smiling weakly.

"Are you sure?" she said pointing a wiggling finger at him and squinting suspiciously.

"Not today."

Being funny was a mistake, the librarian erupted into laughter again, she was laughing so much her glasses had fallen off her head and were now hanging half across her face.

"OK let's see what we have in stock."

She finally stopped laughing and distracted herself with furiously scribbling down the names of the books that were scrolling up the screen in front of her, underlining the ones she thought were most appropriate.

"There you go, that should keep you going!"

"Thanks, wow, that's a lot of books."

"If you need anything else you know who to ask! Mum's the word!" she called across the room as Oscar headed into the rows of books.

One by one he picked the books out and started to build a pile on his desk. There were books of famous cases, crime-solving techniques, handbooks, so many books that Oscar's head was in a spin. After an hour or so of reading, he had filled nearly ten pages of his notebook and was still no clearer about how he should start to investigate the latest crime. He decided that he would go and see Mr Rouse.

The waiting room was empty when he arrived at the opticians.

"Do you have an appointment?" the receptionist asked without looking up from her screen.

"Well...not exactly," replied Oscar.

"What's your name?"

"Oscar Chesterton. I know Mr Rouse."

She looked up but said nothing, unimpressed, just pointed at a seat.

Oscar sat down. *What would a detective do in this situation?* he thought. He probably would have said he had an appointment, or perhaps he would have used some sort of suction cup device to scale the outside of the building and slip in through one of the windows.

Either way, Oscar had already told the receptionist he didn't really have an appointment and he didn't own any climbing gear. He was thinking about leaving when a woman and her daughter came through the security door into reception. The door was one of those heavy types that made a funny breathing noise when it opened and took ages to close. Oscar saw his chance as the receptionist dealt with the other patients and he slipped unnoticed through the door into the sea of corridors that led to Mr Rouse's office. He could vaguely remember the route from the other day. He knew he had to catch the lift, go through the garden and up several flights of stairs. He thought about just shouting out Mr Rouse's name in the hope that he might hear him but he couldn't let anyone else know he was there.

He thought about the receptionist and how she would soon realise what Oscar had done and sound the alarm or worse, call the police. He was about to give up hope when, in the far distance, he saw a glimmer of light. It was the reflection of the golden plaque that hung on the wall outside of Mr Rouse's office. He'd made it. He knocked on the door and waited, listening for any movement in the room, but all was quiet. He knocked again.

"Mr Rouse? It's Oscar Chesterton."

There was no reply. He tried the handle. The door was open.

"Mr Rouse?"

He walked into the room. The old man was sat upright at his desk but didn't turnaround. Oscar moved closer.

"Mr Rouse? It's Oscar."

As he reached the desk, he noticed that Mr Rouse had his eyes closed; he was either asleep or dead. Oscar really hoped it was the first option. He reached out slowly and tapped Mr Rouse on the shoulder, lightly at first and then a little harder. Suddenly, the old man burst into life.

"Hey? Who? Call Scotland Yard! What's going on here then?" he spluttered as he came round.

"Mr Rouse, it's OK, it's me, Oscar! You were asleep. I didn't mean to scare you."

"Me, asleep, no power napping my boy," said the old man as he rubbed the sleep out of his eyes.

"Did we have an appointment?"

"Not really no, but I really need your help. I've landed my first big case and I don't know what to do."

"Solve it, my dear boy, solve it!" Mr Rouse was up now and, after a few agile stretches, he was pacing up and down the room.

"Tell me everything you can about the case? Is it murder in the first?"

"Erm, no, but you're not the first to ask," replied Oscar.

"A famous diamond plucked from the vaults at Lloyds of London?"

"Not quite, but I have come up with a rather good

name for it?"

"An excellent start," said Mr Rouse, "All of the great crimes of this century started with, well a crime, but also a good name."

"I've called it 'The Mystery Victory', for now."

Mr Rouse was suitably impressed; it sort of rhymed. Oscar explained how he had been stuck at first but had found the 'Problem Solving' mode on the glasses and used it to help him come up with the name.

"A true detective investigates every avenue! I'd forgotten about that function," exclaimed Mr Rouse. He shuffled over to the bookcase in the corner, pulled out a rather large book, blew the dust off the cover and handed it to Oscar. The book was entitled 'The Detectives Guide to Being a Detective and Detecting.'

Catchy title, thought Oscar. He read further down, noticed the author had a very familiar name: Rouse.

"You wrote this?"

"I did indeed. It took nearly ten years of my life but it was worth every minute," boasted the old man. "That book contains everything you need to know about solving crime," he continued. "If you promise to take care of it, you can borrow it."

"I promise I'll look after it," said Oscar, flicking through the first few pages, noticing there was even a chapter on 'Solving Crimes Wearing Spectacles'.

"This is perfect."

"Now, tell me more about this mystery victory?" said Mr Rouse sitting back down. Oscar told him everything: the chickenpox epidemic, Rupert's training regime, the spandex, the fact that every other runner fell, to be more precise, slipped on what should have been rock solid, bone dry ground.

Mr Rouse directed him to chapter three in the book: 'Making an Incident Board'. He flicked through the book until he reached chapter three. On the page, there was an antique style illustration of a man standing in front of a board holding a pointy thing in his hand. The board was covered in red string, maps and photos. Underneath the image was the title 'Building a Criminal Profile.'

"We have an incident board already, I just haven't stuck everything on."

Oscar looked up at the clock. It was nearly one o'clock.

"I'd better go. I told my mum I would be back by lunch," he said, as he got up and headed to the door.

"I think you should use the back door from now on, it's much quicker," said Mr Rouse, "You might like this!" he added, pushing the door open and stepping outside with Oscar. The door closed behind them. On the wall by the back door there was a small box.

"Looks like we have locked ourselves out, doesn't it?"

Oscar studied the door. There was no handle or

any other way of opening it.

"Now, if you stand just there." Mr Rouse positioned Oscar in front of the small box and as he did, the box lit up and scanned Oscar's face. It was the same type of scanner he had seen the other day that had activated the walls and made them turn invisible: a face scanner. The door popped open accompanied by a loud electric buzz.

"Keys to the kingdom," said the old man. "My door is always open. Don't forget your book."

Chapter Nine
By the Book

"Where you off to love?" said Oscar's mum when he got up and headed out the lounge.

"Going to bed."

Oscar's dad lowered his paper and eyed his son for a moment before raising it back up.

"Big day tomorrow?" asked his mum.

"Got some reading to do," he replied, already half way up the stairs.

Oscar was up so early the next day that the birds had only just started to sing. He had set his Yoda alarm for six thirty am. This was no standard alarm; instead of a traditional alarm beep when it went off, it woke you up by saying 'Strong in the force is this one!' or 'Be a Jedi you will!' depending on which setting you chose. Oscar hit the light sabre shaped off-switch before the green plastic Jedi had a chance to finish his first verse.

He washed his face twice to wake himself up. He had been up all night reading under his duvet by torchlight. He managed to read most of the book Mr Rouse had given him and had written pages and pages of notes about how to map out his latest investigation. He had so much stuff to carry to HQ that he had piled it all up in a wheelbarrow just to get it down the garden. He had hammers to nail up more boards for his crime scene notes, a ball of red string to pin up between the various boards, pins to stick up his evidence, a tower of cheese sandwiches, a lamp from the spare room (one of the types you often saw on desks in detective movies that swivel round) and, last but not least, the peace lily from the conservatory.

He overheard his dad talking about the importance of good working conditions and decided a plant would be the perfect addition, although he wasn't sure once Mum saw it was missing that he would be able to keep it.

His mum watched from the kitchen window, smiling at her son as he wobbled down the garden with the wheelbarrow. The doorbell rang. It was Jude.

Jude was dressed up as an army officer as he had spilt chocolate milk down the front of his policeman's costume and his mum had made him put it in the wash. Oscar's mum saluted as she beckoned him in.

"Good morning, Jude."

"Captain J if you don't mind," said Jude as he pointed to the army badge on his top.

"Good morning, Captain J. Please accept my sincere apologies."

Jude saluted back immediately, clipping his heels together. Oscar's mum nodded towards the back window, "He's in the shed if you want to go straight out?"

"I think you mean HQ!" said Jude correcting her again before he marched off down the garden. Oscar didn't hear Jude approach; he was too busy nailing the last of his warning signs to the outside of the shed, the one he'd written 'Achtung' on in capital letters that meant danger in German. He had decided that today would be the day that he would tell Jude about Mr Rouse and the spectacular spectacles. He had been waiting for his friend to arrive, playing the conversation over and over in his head. Hammering away, Oscar started to feel like he was being watched. He turned around and almost jumped out of his skin when he spotted Jude standing motionlessly right behind him. Jude had been there for nearly two minutes saluting silently and his arm was beginning to hurt.

"Crikey, Jude, erm I mean, Captain," said Oscar clutching his chest in fright.

"Reporting for duty!" shouted Jude confidently but then immediately looked like he had forgotten something, "Sir?"

"Don't be silly, best friends don't call each other sir and please stop saluting me. We are partners."

This pleased Jude immensely, so much so he almost saluted again. He managed to stop himself at the very last minute by grabbing his arm with his free hand and pulling it back down, *I might have to use that spare string in my pocket to tie it down,* he thought. He was so used to saluting he really wasn't sure he would be able to stop. To distract himself he turned to look at the shed. Oscar noticed him trying to peer inside. "Welcome to HQ! What do you think?"

Jude peered around the door again.

"Go in, have a look round."

Inside the HQ there was a kitchen table, a couple of beanbags and the easel Oscar had, sort of, borrowed from his mum.

Jude was very impressed.

"Nice work!" he said as he worked his way round the shed, tapping tables, crossing his arms, nodding.

"I really like what you've done with the space," he continued. Jude had been ill a couple of weeks back and had been stuck watching interior design shows on TV every day with his mum. After watching so many episodes he had picked up a few of the sayings.

"Do I get my own desk?" asked Jude.

"You can have your own beanbag, how about that?"

Before Oscar even had a chance to turn, Jude had pounced onto his beanbag.

"So, I can take it home with me if it's mine?"

Oscar told him it belonged to the company so no,

he couldn't.

All the banging around had finally woken Watson up and he had managed to slip into HQ unnoticed, taking the last beanbag spot which happened to be conveniently located next to the table with the cheese sandwiches on. *Looks like I got here just in time,* he thought as he snuggled in, pretending to go back to sleep but secretly poised to snatch the sandwiches when the boys weren't looking.

After an hour or so, everything was set up. The boards were ready to be used and half of the cheese sandwiches were gone. Oscar dragged Watson off the beanbag and sat down next to his friend and told him all about the glasses. Jude wasn't sure if he was serious.

"So, you are like a superhero now?" he quizzed. "My best friend is a superhero!"

"Don't be silly, I'm not a superhero."

"You just said you were?"

"No, I said the glasses have special features."

"Do I get any?" asked Jude, hopefully. Watson was thinking something similar but it involved the cheese sandwiches that he was shuffling towards.

Oscar tried to explain that his glasses were particularly spectacular and that he wasn't sure if another pair even existed. Jude's head dropped and he headed for the door.

"But once I have got used to them, I promise I

will let you have a go."

The little soldier still wasn't happy but it stopped him from leaving.

"I'll show you the laser?"

That sealed the deal and Jude jumped back onto his beanbag.

"Could you pass me one of those cheese sandwiches, please?"

Jude pulled himself across to the sandwiches and passed the plate to his friend. Oscar set the sandwich down on the desk next to him and told Jude and Watson to stand well back. When they were all a safe distance away, Oscar pressed the button on the side of the glasses until the word 'Combat' came up on the screen. It had all happened so fast the time he tried on the other laser spectacles and set fire to Mr Rouse's office, but since then the old man had been busy tweaking and now the spectacular spectacles had a proper set of cross hairs that came up on the lenses to help aim. The target locked onto the unsuspecting snack and the word 'armed' came up. Oscar fired the laser at the sandwich for a split second and then quickly thought, *Stop*.

He turned round. Jude and Watson were both stood silently, their mouths wide open. Jude was pointing at the smoking sandwich which now resembled a lump of coal more than a tasty meal. Watson didn't care, he was dribbling at the smell of the cooked cheese in the air.

"You see, we need to be careful, they can be very

dangerous," insisted Oscar.

"Cheese toasties aren't dangerous?" said a confused Jude.

"No, of course the toastie isn't dangerous; I mean the glasses!"

It took a while longer for Oscar to convince his friend that the glasses were for restricted use only, but they finally moved on when he presented Jude with a pair of his mum's sunglasses (that were now fixed to Jude's face with red string as they kept slipping off his nose).

"Right, let's get down to business," said Oscar, as he leafed through the book Mr Rouse had given him to find the chapter on 'crime maps'.

"What's 'The Myz-tery Vic-tori'?" asked Jude, attempting to read the words that were on the main board.

"This is what we are going to find out. It's our first real case."

Chapter Ten
The Scene of the Crime

School was now closed for the summer and the gates at the back of the playing fields were locked. Jude said that he had heard there was a hole in the fence that some of the big kids sneaked out of at lunchtime.

"Go find it boy!" said Oscar, letting the dog off the lead. Watson knew this was important and managed to ignore the lure of an old crisp packet and the remnants of a sausage roll as he hunted, nose to the ground, for the hole in the fence. *Be professional,* he thought, doing his best to keep on the trail. It didn't take long; a minute later he was back barking at them to follow him.

"Good boy, Watson. Now show us the way."

The boys followed, crouched down as if they were escaping from a prisoner of war camp, dodging the spotlights. Not that they were hidden, anyone could have seen them or, for that matter, heard them as Watson was standing by the hole barking at the two friends.

"Quiet Watson, remember we are on a secret mission!" whispered Oscar as they reached the hole, it was much larger than the boys had thought it would be, in fact it was almost as big as a car.

The three detectives stood together at the start line of the one hundred metre track. Whilst Jude tried to fix the oversized sunglasses back onto his face, Oscar put on the spectacular spectacles and switched them on. The lenses came to life as Oscar clicked his way through to 'Search' mode.

Oscar hadn't had them in search mode before and it took him a moment to adjust as his vision became like a computer game, as if he was looking through graph paper; the sky, the grass, even Watson, was now divided into small squares. He was going to try and explain to Jude what he was seeing but thought it would be a good opportunity to let his friend try them on.

"OK, so remember, try not to think anything to do with lasers and if you do then think 'stop' straight away," said Oscar as he handed the younger boy his spectacles.

"Copy that!" said Jude, screwing his face up as he tried to stop his brain from thinking about lasers and cheese toasties. He carefully slipped on the glasses, determined to control his mind. For a moment, he could see the grid that Oscar had been talking about, right before the words 'Cheese Toastie' popped into his head like a big bubble quickly followed by the word 'Laser'. 'Combat' mode flashed up immediately. Jude turned slowly to Oscar, a panicked look on his face.

"What's wrong?"

"I told you I needed a snack before we came out," Jude said as he closed his eyes and hoped the glasses would stop reading his mind.

"I can't stop thinking about cheese toasties!"

"Jude!"

The red beams shot out, scorching the grass in front of Jude's feet. Oscar dived onto the floor as Jude swung around and the beam shot over his head.

"Quick, think 'stop'!" yelled Oscar.

"Stop!" shouted Jude.

"Don't shout it, think it!" shouted Oscar even louder.

Oscar took his hands off his head and looked up; there was no sign of laser beams anywhere. Jude's shoulders had dropped and his bottom lip started to judder. The shouting had got so loud that Jude had stopped thinking altogether and instead had started to cry. Oscar saw his chance and grabbed the glasses off Jude's face. That was when he noticed how much he had upset his friend.

"Hey, don't cry big man," said Oscar, placing his hand lightly on his friend's shoulder. "I didn't mean to scare you. I didn't know what else to do."

Jude wasn't ready to speak to him yet; he was too busy sniffing and wiping his nose.

"Look, how about I put you in charge of the evidence board?"

Jude raised his head slightly but still wouldn't look at his friend. Oscar took his rucksack off and put it down on the floor so he could have a good rummage around. He pulled out his mum's camera.

"You can be the official crime photographer too."

This was enough and Jude was back on side. Oscar put the spectacles back on and clicked through to 'Search' mode. Underneath the word search there were several other words: replay, outlines, lie detector and photo. He didn't want to take Jude's new job away so he steered away from 'photo' but thought he would try 'Replay'. A whirring noise started when he selected the new mode, promptly followed by the two small probes sliding out of both of the top corners of the frames of his glasses. The word 'replay' was replaced by the words 'memory bank' on the lenses.

He cast his mind back to Sports Day and, as he did, images from the day started to appear. It was more like a hologram than a photograph and the more Oscar thought about the day, the clearer the images became.

"Quick, Jude we need to get to the start of lane five."

The two boys ran to the far end of the starting line. Jude was puzzled as to why they had started running but did it anyway. Oscar could now see a crystal-clear vision of the past playing out on the lenses of his glasses in perfect time with his memories. It was so realistic that he jumped back when the hologram of Rupert bent down next to him under starter's orders.

"On your marks," said Oscar, as he pictured the start of the race. He looked up and down the starting line and there were all the other runners getting ready to go. He was so focused he didn't notice Jude was bending down with them, thinking the two of them were about to have a race.

"Bang!" shouted Oscar as he watched the holographic Mr Hudson fire the starting gun. Oscar started to jog just behind the runners, watching carefully, waiting for the first boy to fall. In the distance, he could see Jude, hurtling across the finishing line and stretching out into his first dab.

Oscar looked to his left as the boy from the red team started to lose his footing. He squinted to get a better view of where the boy's feet first departed from the ground. The spectacles responded to the eye movement and adjusted focus accordingly, zooming in on the track and then pausing the playback, a big pause icon flashed up in the corner of the lens.

"Jude, stop dabbing and come here!" shouted Oscar as he ran over to the frozen, floating red team runner. The playback paused just as both feet left the floor. Jude joined his crouching friend, closely followed by Watson. Oscar rubbed the ground beneath the holographic athlete, turned his hand over to reveal a layer of mud.

"Mud!"

Jude was unimpressed and slightly miffed his dabbing had been interrupted. Watson sniffed Oscar's hand in case it was food. He licked a tiny bit off, rolling it around on his tongue.

"No Watson, it's evidence!" said Oscar, pulling his hand away.

Evidence doesn't taste very nice, thought Watson, so he ate some grass to get rid of the taste.

"I knew there was something fishy!" said Oscar proudly as he stood up and started to make his way to the next runner. *Play*, he thought, the holographic playback continued.

All three detectives jogged along together as Oscar watched the green team runner, Jude always a stride ahead; he was very competitive. The green team runner's left leg started to wobble; he was almost up to the same place on the track as where the red runner fell. The green team runner went down face first. Oscar paused the replay just as the runner's feet left the floor. The runner looked pretty comical (it was quite hard not to laugh) like a rocket about to take off or a swimmer preparing to dive into a swimming pool. Oscar touched the earth beneath the frozen runner then lifted his muddy hand triumphantly.

"Quick, Jude, go to the next lane and check for mud."

Jude shuffled off and rubbed his hand on the ground; there was mud.

"Mud?" said Jude, with a confused look on his

face. Oscar instructed his friend to take pictures of each lane where the mud was, explaining his thoughts about the mysterious wet patches.

"Don't you see? Each of the runner's lanes have these patches of mud where they fell," he began, walking over to Rupert's lane and standing next to the unlikely holographic winner of the race. He rubbed his hand on the floor in line with where the other runners had fallen. There was just dust, baked dirt from the recent heat wave.

"Yeah, it's the ground. It's made of mud and dirt?" quizzed Jude.

"It's elementary, my dear boy," quoted Oscar.

"Ele… what?"

"Elementary, it means simple… I think." Oscar wiped his dirty hand on his jeans. "Someone sabotaged the race."

Chapter Eleven
The Unusual Suspects

Back at HQ, Oscar was busy setting up all the evidence on the boards. He had drawn a map of the school field marking out all the possible exits and entrances. He was pretty pleased with it. Using replay on his spectacles, he had even managed to draw quite a few of the crowd but had decided against sketching everyone when he realised there were probably over two hundred people there.

He'd settled on splitting the field into coloured blocks: parents, teachers and runners. He had run out of green pen due to the amount of grass he had coloured in so the last few bits, including the one hundred-metre track, were coloured blue. On the track he had drawn white lines, like they do at murder scenes, marking where each runner had fallen.

The knock on the door almost made him stick one of his pins straight into his pinky as he tried to pin his completed map on the evidence board. He crept up to the door silently and peeked through the peephole.

There was nobody there.

"Who goes there?" said Oscar, in his most threatening voice.

"It's Jude."

Oscar got up onto his tiptoes and at that height he could see just a red hood. "What's the password?" said Oscar.

"Erm. Monkey nuts?"

"Nope but I like it."

"You never told me the password, but you know it's me."

"How?"

"Because I'm your best friend?"

This was indeed true, as was the fact that there was no password. Every HQ needed a password though and coming up with one became the first mission of the day. Oscar unlocked the door. He had locked it as the HQ had become the official crime lab and he didn't want any interruptions unless they involved more sandwiches or cake. Jude looked around at all the boards that were now covered with notes, sketches and red string. There was almost a web of red cotton around the room linking up all the different types of evidence.

Oscar motioned for his friend to sit down and it was only at this point he noticed that the red hood he had seen outside was part of Jude's outfit of the day. Today Jude was dressed like a ninja.

"Nice outfit Jude," said Oscar, standing back to take in his friend's look in its entirety.

"Actually, it's Red Ninja today," said Jude.

"So I see," confirmed Oscar, "Are those…?"

"My trusty nunchucks? Yes." Jude slowly drew them from his belt. "Please stand well back; this could get crazy."

The younger boy started slowly at first, twisting the nunchucks in each hand making his own swooshing noises to make it seem like they were going faster. It actually looked more like breakdancing than Ninjitsu. The display came to a sharp end when he hit himself in the face with one of the sticks and decided to sit back down.

"I've got it!" cried Oscar. Jude raised his eyebrow questioningly, which hurt a bit as it was where he had just hit himself with the nunchuck.

"The new password is breakdancing ninja!"

Jude loved it that much he had to have his nunchucks momentarily confiscated before he destroyed HQ completely, flying around shouting the password.

Oscar had fashioned himself a pointer out of an old piece of bamboo from his dad's greenhouse. It was the perfect length and made a great swishing noise not dissimilar to the one Jude had made to add dramatic effect when putting on his ninja show.

"So, as you can see, I have drawn up a list of prime suspects," he said, whipping his pointer up and down the list of the three names. The prime suspects were Rupert, Rupert's dad and Mr Hudson the PE teacher.

"Rupert is an obvious one," Oscar said drawing a big red circle around the name, "A. We know that Rupert trained hard. B. We know he had very tight running shorts that he could hardly move in. C. We know that he was the slowest runner on the field. Ergo…"

"Hergo?"

"Ergo."

"Eeegoo?"

"ERGO!" blurted out Oscar. "It's a posh word for 'so there it is'. It doesn't matter, all I am trying to say is, D. He could never have won the race without some form of help."

"A rocket pack, perhaps?" said Jude, screwing his face up and looking sneaky.

"A rocket pack?"

"You know, like James Bond."

"I know what a rocket pack is but I also know that Rupert's specialist running gear was so tight he could barely breathe, so where would he have concealed a rocket pack?"

"Hergo!" said Jude, proudly, "He has a very teeny, weeny, whiny one?"

Jude took out his crime notebook and wrote down the name *Rupert* next to the number one, followed by a very small sketch of a rocket pack.

"There was no tiny rocket pack."

"But…"

"No buts and no rockets," said Oscar more firmly

this time. "Somehow though, if indeed he is guilty, he did cheat!"

Now it was all coming back to Jude. He crossed out his rocket pack sketch and instead wrote *wet patch* and showed it to Oscar, smiling mischievously.

"Yes, my sniggering ninja, one of these suspects has a wet patch and we will find out which one."

Even though Oscar planned to go round and interrogate Rupert, he did have his doubts about him being the mastermind behind the crime. He had watched Rupert trying to tie his laces up only last week after PE; he ended up tying them together after a number of attempts and, even though he could see what he had done, he tried to walk off. He quickly stepped back to the board and wrote next to Rupert's name 'Criminal Mastermind' followed by three large question marks.

"Rupert is not exactly the smartest cookie is he?"

"That's not very nice," said Jude.

"Neither is crime, my friend," replied Oscar gravely. "No, this crime was done by a professional and I don't think Rupert falls into that category, but let's see."

Oscar picked up the book Mr Rouse had lent him and flicked through. He had marked lots of the pages with little stickers. He turned to the page that had the header 'Inside Job'.

"It may well have been an inside job according to this."

Jude scribbled everything down. Oscar could see his friend was confused. He read aloud from the book.

"An inside job is a crime committed by, or with the assistance of, a person living or working on the premises where it occurred."

This was too much for Jude to write down so he just underlined the word 'inside' a couple of times and doodled another little rocket pack. He had decided he would have to solve this crime using ninja magic as opposed to notes, and that he wanted a rocket pack for Christmas. He wrote down 'must learn ninja magic' and drew a big circle around the words.

"This could mean that Mr Hudson was involved. Rupert's victory meant that his house won the overall Sports Day which would give him what they call the 'motivation' to commit the crime." Oscar wrote down the word *motivation* underneath each of the suspects.

"This leaves us with Rupert's dad. Now, this is an obvious one too."

Oscar thought back to how he had seen Rupert stumbling through the park each morning trying to keep up with his dad on his electric bike. He also thought back to the end of the race and how Rupert's dad had almost fallen over celebrating as he ran, crab like, up and down the line of shocked parents. He seemed to remember that he was also holding up his hands as if they were pistols and firing off imaginary victory shots.

Oscar went over to a box in the corner and started rummaging around. He pulled out two hats and an old coat that belonged to his dad. It was too big really, came down to Oscar's feet. He passed one of the hats to Jude who span it around in his hands like a pancake. There was a card tucked in the rim. He spelt the word written on it out in his head, *'P-r-e-s-s'*. He looked to his friend for an explanation.

"It's our cover. We are going to pass ourselves off as writers for the local newspaper, reporting on the school sports day."

Jude put the hat on carefully, making sure it didn't totally cover up his ninja hood.

"We are going deep undercover!" he cried. Oscar whistled and Watson appeared at the door. He tucked in one of the 'press' labels he had made into Watson's collar.

"Watson, you are now officially our press-hound."

No, I'm not! thought Watson. *I'm a Beagle.*

Chapter Twelve
Rupert the Genius

It took much longer than they expected to get round to Rupert's house as their hats kept blowing off as they rode along. Oscar decided in future they would need to get hats with straps to keep them on in case they ever needed to make a quick escape, chase suspects down or ride anywhere in the rain.

As they pulled up on the drive they noticed the garage door was opening.

"Quick Jude, hide in the bush!"

It was only a small bush so it was quite cramped.

"Why are we hiding?" whispered Jude.

"Be quiet will you!"

The garage door opened and Rupert's dad slowly backed his car out onto the drive.

"Quick, take some pictures!" Oscar ordered as he shoved the camera towards his friend. Jude held the camera up and pressed the button, but nothing happened; he hadn't turned it on.

By the time he was ready to take a picture, Rupert's dad was already half way up the road. He took a few pictures of the car in the distance, one of a chimney stack, a flock of birds, a drain and quite a few of the bush.

"You can stop now Jude."

The car had disappeared around the corner. They straightened themselves up, their heads poking up over the bush, only to realise Watson had disappeared too. Oscar whistled for him but the only response was a rustle from another nearby bush. Watson had found some hidden treasure, a discarded bit of a sausage or something. Oscar tugged him out by the collar and gave him a stern telling off.

"We are on duty Watson!"

Watson looked down at his front paws in shame. Oscar told him he would be left at home if he ran off again. Watson thought it was worth getting told off for the nice piece of sausage that was now balanced perfectly on his tongue waiting for the moment when Oscar was distracted so he could swallow it.

Rupert's mum answered the door in her cooking apron. She didn't look very happy about being disturbed.

"Yes?"

"Hello Mrs Walker, we are from the local paper and we are hoping to interview Rupert about his Sports Day victory."

"It's not really a convenient time right now. I'm right in the middle of cooking," she said, wiping her hands on her apron before staring suspiciously at the two detectives in disguise. "Are you sure you're from the paper?"

They both nodded.

"That's funny because we already had someone come round from one of the papers."

Oscar looked at Jude, Jude looked at Oscar, Watson looked at both of them, still trying to secretly swallow the remains of the sausage. Jude, thinking on his feet, whipped out his notepad.

"That's because we are from the school paper."

"Oh, I see, I didn't know the school had its own paper."

Buoyed by his friend's invention, Oscar jumped in.

"It's very new. In fact, Rupert will be the cover star of the first edition."

Rupert's mum was suitably impressed and beckoned them in.

"We have company Rupert!" she shouted to her son. Oscar and Jude peered around her to see if he was coming but there was no sign of him. Rupert's mum rolled her eyes and shouted for him again, this time going to the bottom of the stairs. There was still no response.

"Rupert Walker get down these stairs right now!" screeched his mother so loudly that it made both the boys jump. Watson was so scared he almost spat out the last bit of his sausage.

There was a thump from somewhere in the house followed by heavy footsteps banging down the stairs. Rupert appeared at the door. He was still in his pyjamas.

"I thought I told you to get dressed."

Rupert's eyes stayed fixed on his feet.

"Hey Rupert," said Oscar, trying to change the subject.

"Rupert, these nice boys have come round to interview you for the school paper," said Rupert's mum as she motioned for Oscar and Jude to sit down. "So, maybe you need to get dressed before they take your picture. Why don't you go upstairs and wash your face, put that nice shirt on we got you for your holiday and grab your medal whilst you're up there? I think it's in your dad's office."

Oscar and Jude sat down at the kitchen table as Rupert's mum put Watson in the garden with their dog Dutch.

"Why don't you go and play with little Dutchy?" she said, shoving Watson out into the garden. But as she shut the door, Watson saw that playtime was already over before it had begun. At the bottom of the garden stood one of the largest dogs Watson had ever seen: a black and white Great Dane. He was in fact the largest breed in the world and he didn't look very pleased to see Watson.

"Easy now there, big fella!" Watson barked desperately.

Back in the kitchen, the boys didn't hear their friend's cry for help. The Walkers had recently had double glazed windows fitted that blocked out nearly all the noise from outside, even dogs barking.

"Would you boys like a glass of milk?"

"No thank you, Mrs Walker. I never drink on duty," replied Oscar. Jude said he would have a small glass as it was nearly lunchtime.

"Here's my little champion," she said as Rupert entered the room, before she noticed he hadn't tucked his shirt in and busied herself adjusting Rupert's clothing until his trousers were pulled up so far you could see the tops of his socks.

Oscar placed his notebook on the table in front of him, quickly opening it when he realized it had 'We Are Detectives' written on the cover. Jude checked that he had turned the camera on properly this time.

"Do you mind if we take a few photographs to go with the story?"

Rupert shrugged and Jude set about snapping away.

"Sit up Rupert, shoulders back, smile."

She's like the bossiest mum in the world, thought Oscar, feeling sorry for Rupert as he watched him try to smile between her orders and the camera flash that blinded him each time it went off.

"So, well done on winning the big race. You must be very happy."

Rupert almost managed a smile that time, only to be caught at the last minute by another blinding flash.

"We just have a few questions for you, if that's OK?"

"I guess."

"Erm, OK great…" Oscar was a bit stuck; he had never interrogated anyone before.

"I know you did a lot of preparation for the race but we were wondering what exactly you did on the actual day?"

Rupert pointed over to the fridge. There was a training plan stuck on it with some fridge magnets. Jude took a quick snap.

"His father wrote him his very own training programme. Every day, he was up at five and running round the park before school," said Rupert's mum, trying to encourage Rupert to start speaking. "I thought it was great, got him out of that room for once."

"I didn't realise your dad was a fitness trainer?"

"He's not," replied Rupert. "He just reads the magazines."

"His father used to be a semi-professional footballer actually," added Mrs Walker proudly.

Rupert was now blinking incessantly as the flash went off again and again.

"That's probably enough pictures," Oscar suggested, smiling at his friend whilst trying to secretly nod at him to stop and sit down. Jude turned the camera over to see how to switch it off accidently taking a picture of himself, the flash blinding him momentarily. With big white lights pinging around his blinking eyes, he felt his way back to his seat and put the camera down.

"I meant on the actual day of the race, was there anything special? Anything out of the ordinary?"

"My dad asked me to wash the car."

"That's not exactly strange, is it?" added his mum.

Oscar darted a look at Jude. In his head, Oscar had started to build a picture of what might have happened on the day of the race. If Rupert was washing a car that morning, wasn't it feasible he could have sneaked away from his driveway with the hose in tow and headed up to the school?

The Walkers lived so close to the school he would have easily been able to run an extra long hose from the house all the way to the field. Oscar tried to picture it; Rupert slipping across the road, hose in hand, waiting for a car to pass and then scurrying through the hole in the fence that they had discovered the other day.

"Does your dad, by any chance, have a particularly long hose?"

At this, Rupert's mum raised her eyebrows, bemused by the line of questioning.

"He just got a new one with an extension," replied Rupert.

"Does it have one of those squirty guns?" said Jude, joining in on the line of questioning.

"Yes."

"That is sooo cool."

"I guess."

Oscar ignored the chat; he was too busy furiously scribbling in his pad: Rupert plus hose equals crime solved, then the word 'guilty'. He slid the pad sneakily across the table to Jude. It took him a few moments to get through the words. It was only when he reached the word 'guilty' written in big capitals that he caught up; he readied his concealed nunchucks in case Rupert didn't want to come quietly.

"So, you washed the car and then what happened?"

"I didn't say I washed it!"

Oscar was confused. He pulled his pad back from Jude and flicked back to his last note.

"You clearly said you washed the car?"

"He was going to wash the car but we couldn't find the hose!"

"I thought you said he had just got a new fancy one?" pressed Oscar.

"Things are always disappearing in this house," said Rupert's mum.

"But just so we are clear, you are currently hose-less?"

"Without hose?" added Jude.

"No hose in the house?"

Rupert and his mum were both looking suspiciously at their guests now. The interview came to an abrupt end once the cake landed on the table.

"Would you boys like a slice?"

Rupert's hand scrabbled across the table but, just as he was about to strike at the cake, his mum dragged it away from him.

"It's for the guests, Rupert, not you!"

Both boys felt mean taking cake when Rupert wasn't allowed any so they said thanks and prepared to leave.

"I have something else that might be good for your paper." said Rupert blocking the door. Oscar was keen to leave before their cover was blown.

"Please."

"Well we are always on the hunt for a good story." said Oscar motioning for Rupert to lead the way.

"Keep your eyes open," he whispered to Jude just incase it was a trap. Jude readied his nunchucks under his coat as Rupert opened the door, not sure if there was a trap waiting for them. Nothing could have prepared them for what was in the room.

Most of the space was taken up by Lego. You could hardly see any of the furniture there was so much Lego in the room. Even the bedspread was covered in Lego characters. Taking pride of place in the middle of the room was a large table. There was clearly a significant construction going on but it was covered with a blanket, which Rupert promptly pulled off like a magician on TV.

"I thought maybe you could take a picture of this for

your paper?"

"Wow! How long did this take?" said Oscar. "It's incredible." Jude could hardly speak he was so impressed.

"Flip!" he exclaimed.

Rupert had reconstructed Sports Day out of Lego, right down to the crowd waving their arms in the air. Rupert picked one of the figures from the table.

"That's me."

He had even managed to build a tiny medal out of a Lego. Oscar shot Jude a look, Jude shot one back, not entirely sure why.

"Can you keep a secret?"

Rupert crossed his heart. At that, Oscar ripped his coat off. Jude followed suit.

"We are not really reporters, we are detectives!"

Rupert looked slightly disappointed, "So I won't be in the school paper?"

"We just made that up!" said Jude as he whipped out his nunchucks. "We are detective masterminds!"

"And we would like to offer you a place in the organisation," added Oscar.

"But I'm not very clever so you should probably find someone else."

Oscar put his arm around the boy, pointing toward his Lego creation.

"Then what's this?"

"Lego?"

"No, my friend, this is magnificent."

"A masterpiece!" added Jude. Oscar put his hand down outstretched in the middle of the three of them; he'd seen them do it at American football matches. Jude quickly placed his on top. Both of the boys looked at Rupert, his hand poised nervously above theirs.

"Join us?"

Rupert closed his eyes and slammed his hand down.

Chapter Thirteen
Back to the Drawing Board

Oscar had to admit that Rupert's apparent innocence was a blow but the fact that they had discovered Rupert's secret talent, and a new member of the bureau, went some way to make up for the disappointment.

He had assumed that they had managed to solve the crime in record time. He had pictured himself, Jude and Watson all dressed in 'monkey' suits as his dad called them; posh black and white suits with bow ties and shoes, so shiny, you could see your face in them. Watson obviously didn't have shoes on but he did have a rather fetching bow tie collar. They were attending the annual awards ceremony for crime fighting. They had been nominated in the category 'Fastest Detectives in the World', and they had won.

The crowd rose to its feet, the whoops and bravos getting louder and louder. Jude couldn't resist one little dab as he reached the stage. Oscar stopped him just as he started his moonwalk. Yes, they had made it, they were at the top of the detective world, the crème de la crème, the Bee's knees; TV deals and books were surely next. *But what's that smell?* he thought, so pungent that it had burst the little dream bubble he was in. The award, the suits, the applause all faded. He was back at the side of the road outside Rupert's house. He looked at his red ninja friend and Watson, and was about to say let's go, when he noticed that Watson had done a poo right at the end of the Walker's recently laid driveway and Oscar hadn't brought any bags with him. *I bet this doesn't happen to Superman*, he thought.

"We'll try again tomorrow!" Oscar proclaimed as he watched his crestfallen friend shuffle off home. He was putting his bike away when he heard Jude call after him.

"If at first you don't succeed try, try and try again my nan always says."

He rounded his wisdom off with one last dab.

"No retreat, no surrender!" Oscar fired back. This was something he had heard in a Kung Fu movie.

Jude rubbed his chin thinking about another motto to encourage his pal, but nothing popped up.

"Remember the Alamo!" shouted Jude.

Oscar smiled; he had no idea what it meant but he liked it all the same. *I couldn't ask for a better friend,* he thought, "You're the best!" he shouted back.

Jude was about to say something else he had heard his nan say but his mum called him in as it was getting dark, so he thought he would save it for another time.

Oscar was going to go and spend some time back at HQ, get everything ready for the next day's investigation, but he decided to watch Arsenal play Liverpool instead. His dad was home and sometimes a cuddle from his dad was all he needed.

The disappointment of Rupert's innocence had faded and been replaced with a sense of relief. He had seen Rupert training in the park every day; tried his best. *Maybe this isn't such a crime?* he thought, *Let him have his victory*! Oscar was glad that Rupert was having his time in the spotlight and that he was now their official 'Crime Scene Master Builder', but he couldn't shrug the feeling that there was still something fishy about the whole affair.

That night he had a dream. He was pushing a trolley along in the supermarket. Everyone that worked there he recognised from Sports Day. The athletes that had fallen over in the hundred metres were behind the cheese counter with those funny nets on their heads. Oscar watched the caretaker from school (he was a trolley collector, even had one of those high visibility jackets on) pushing a never-ending row of trolleys out of the store. Oscar looked down at his own trolley; he could hardly push, it was so heavy. The bread aisle was on a steep hill and he was rolling back towards a bottomless sea of blueberries. *Why is this so hard?* he thought. He looked up at his trolley expecting it to be full of heavy shopping but instead, there was Superman; he was sitting in the baby seat at the front. It was a bit of a squeeze, but he looked much happier than he had in the last dream. Oscar couldn't stop the trolley slipping backwards. *Maybe Superman needed to go on a diet like his Aunty Sheila was always on?* he thought. He was very heavy.

"Don't give up!" said the strange infant version of the visitor from another planet.

"It's too heavy!"

"Use the force!" came another familiar voice. Oscar peered around Superman and saw that his Yoda alarm clock had come to life and was now waving at him from the compartment at the end of the trolley where his mum always kept the bags.

Oscar dug his heels in and, as he did, suddenly the gradient of the hill changed direction, like the whole thing was a giant seesaw. He jumped on the trolley as it sped off down the hill. They were going fast now; they picked up Jude near the freezers where they kept the ice cream. Watson, wearing a pair of skiing goggles, leapt on with a string of sausages trailing out of his mouth. Everyone was happy, they all laughed, even when they crashed into a big pile of toilet rolls. Oscar woke with a thump. He laughed so much he had fallen out of bed. At first he struggled to make sense of the strange dream but as he stared into the brown milk of his Coco Pops he remembered his friends words of encouragement. *No retreat, no surrender!* he thought.

After the disappointment of the previous day, Oscar had decided it was time to introduce Jude to Mr Rouse. As they rode along, he explained that Mr Rouse was similar to Q in James Bond but instead of cars and exploding pens he developed spectacular spectacles. This had started Jude on one of his questioning moments.

"Can we ask him for one of those cars that go under water?"

"No."

"What about a watch we can speak to?"

"He just does glasses."

"OK, a rocket pack? He must have one of those."

"He probably has got one of those, but mainly he just does glasses. Now, please be quiet I'm trying to perfect my bunny hop."

Oscar told Jude to tell his mum they were going to the skate park to give them enough time to go to see Mr Rouse and get back without anyone noticing. Jude didn't like lying to his mum but this was business. Unfortunately, the only way he could lie to his mum was by crossing his fingers and shutting his eyes. This usually gave it away but for some reason she had let him go, as long as he was back to see his grandma later.

"Is she bringing cake?" Jude enquired.

"Yes."

"Deal."

As they approached the big mirrored building with the large pair of spectacles hanging on the sign over the door, Jude started to worry.

"What if I'm going blind?" he asked his friend.

"Well, let's test it. Can you see?"

"Yes, but don't you have to be blind to go to the opticians?"

"At least you know if you are going to get glasses, they will probably shoot missiles or…"

"Make ice cream?" Jude interrupted him.

"Possibly."

"Help me, I'm blind!" shouted Jude, shutting his eyes and narrowly missing a nearby bush.

They both laughed.

"I think you will be fine," Oscar assured him.

Jude's outfit of the day was a 'cool dude'. This consisted of sunglasses, even though it was raining, a leather jacket, a T-shirt with a green furry monster playing the guitar and the words, '*Rock till you drop*' written in letters that looked like boulders. There was always a knock on behavioural effect when Jude put on an outfit, and today's included a lot of air guitar and calling everyone 'dude'. The small detective had even called Oscar's mum a dude when he arrived that morning at the house. Oscar asked him if he could refrain from calling Mr Rouse a dude as he wasn't sure that he would understand what it meant.

They pulled up by the back door and chained their bikes to a nearby road sign. Oscar told Jude to stand back as he stood in front of the small box on the wall and, sure enough, the box came to life, scanned Oscar's eyes and the door promptly clicked open. Jude tried to do it too but he couldn't reach the box so he just waved at it and pretended it had worked. Once they were inside, it seemed that maybe Mr Rouse wasn't there. The office looked deserted.

"Mr Rouse? It's Oscar."

There was no reply.

"I brought my friend Jude to meet you. I hope you don't mind."

"You can call me 'Dude' or 'Doctor Rock' if you want," Jude added.

Oscar was about to suggest they leave when he noticed the front door to the office was ajar. Jude had found his way to the big black seat in the middle of the room and was trying to spin himself round. Oscar left him to it and stealthily made his way to the front door of the office. He pushed the door open and, as he did, a small, white, dimpled, ball rolled past on the carpet. He poked his head out of the door and looked down the endless corridor. In the distance he could see a collection of white balls. He looked the other way, squinting, and right down the end of the corridor, he spotted a small colourful figure.

"Mr Rouse?" he called out.

The distant figure waved back at him and a minute later another white ball rolled past Oscar's feet. He looked back up the corridor and could now make out it was Mr Rouse, but he was wearing a very strange outfit. He had socks on up to his knees and a very colourful jumper covered in diamonds.

Mr Rouse was practising his golf. Oscar walked towards him, carefully stepping over the golf balls that littered the corridor.

"Dear boy, how are you? I didn't expect to see you today. I'm just polishing up my putting skills for the annual 'Optometrist's Gold' golf tournament this weekend. Care to join me?"

Oscar said he didn't play golf but he did need some crime fighting help as the investigation they were working on had hit a bit of a speed bump.

"Step into my office," said the old man as he ushered Oscar back through the office door. As soon as the old man stepped through the door, Jude jumped out of the seat and began his air guitar salute.

"Whassup dude!" shouted Jude, completely forgetting Oscar's request not to address the old man that way.

"Dude!" replied Mr Rouse surprisingly, launching into a brief moment of air guitar before clearing his throat and introducing himself properly.

"I'm guessing you must be Jude the Dude?" he said as they shook hands formally.

"My friends call me Dr Rock."

"A pleasure to meet you...Dr Rock."

Oscar explained that Jude was his official partner in crime- solving and that they had recently hired an amazing crime scene builder who had initially been their main suspect. Mr Rouse seemed pleased; he listed off a number of famous detectives who worked with partners and stressed that three heads were definitely better than one.

Mr Rouse thought it would be a good idea to start by showing Jude the spectacle library. Oscar was still amazed at all the different types of spectacles, but Jude had become fixated with one pair in particular.

"Yes, you have found the old Ninjitsu specs. I picked those up in a little place called Nagasaki. Would you like to try them on?"

Jude explained that he had been a ninja the day before so he thought he would be able to handle them. Mr Rouse took them out of the display and handed them to the young detective.

"Now, maybe it's best you stand in the middle of the room; give yourself some space."

Jude moved to the middle of the room and slipped them on. They were the same as Oscar's glasses in the fact that there was a small button behind the ear that activated them. The main difference though was that when he pressed the button on the side of the glasses they extended themselves in a strap around the back of Jude's head.

"You might feel a tightness at the back of your head for a moment. Don't worry, it's just the neural brain trigger," continued Mr Rouse. Jude was listening. On one lens appeared the word Attack and on the other Defence.

"Blink to choose."

Of course, Jude chose attack. Instantly his arms raised up and he performed three quick punches. He blinked again and this time launched into several kicks.

"I'm a ninja!" shouted Jude. Each time he blinked he performed another move perfectly.

"I think your friend may have found his calling, a true ninja dude," said Mr Rouse to Oscar, who was patiently waiting to discuss the case.

"Right, how can I help you with this case?" enquired the old man as Jude continued to attack his imaginary opponents around the room.

Oscar explained that they had drawn up a list of suspects and that within minutes of questioning the first one they thought they had solved the crime. Mr Rouse assured him that crime was always about elimination to some degree and to not get disheartened at the first hurdle.

Rupert had what Mr Rouse called an, 'alibi'. This meant that Rupert could not be responsible for the crime as he was at home with his mother in the run up to the race and the fact that he was 'hose-less' only added to his alibi.

Oscar said it was all fine anyway as Rupert had now joined forces with them. This made Mr Rouse raise an eyebrow.

"He is a Lego genius. We need him."

Mr Rouse asked Oscar why he had chosen the other two as suspects.

"Well, I guess because it made sense. I read about motivation in the book you lent me and they were the only two other people who have some of it," said Oscar.

"All good deductions, my boy. Excellent work," Mr Rouse said. "Now, all you have to do is make sure you have the facts before you go after the next suspect."

"I think I have those," said Oscar.

The two of them looked back into the spectacle library. Jude was still kicking and punching around the room. He was still kicking and punching when they left. Mr Rouse offered to give him the spectacles if he took care of them and didn't wear them all the time.

"Cowabunga!" said Jude.

"Indeed," said Mr Rouse. The old man paused for a second, "You might have to keep a few secrets from your new friend Rupert if his dad is a suspect."

"Roger that!" said Oscar. Jude wasn't so sure about lying, but Oscar assured him it was just to protect the innocent.

Back at HQ, Oscar confiscated the ninja glasses from Jude and put them on the top shelf with the paints where he couldn't reach, not because he was being mean, he was just worried about Jude injuring himself. Initially, this had made Jude quite sulky but Oscar assured him that whenever they needed some extra muscle, he would let him have them back. Oscar also called Rupert and asked if he could bring the Lego crime scene over to help them with the investigation.

"Right, we need to look at the facts before Rupert gets here."

Jude begrudgingly took out his notebook, keeping one eye on where Oscar had placed the ninja spectacles.

He wrote down the word 'facts', but spelt it 'fax'. Oscar thought about what happened with Rupert; he hadn't had access to a hose so he couldn't have sabotaged the track. This also eliminated Rupert's dad in Oscar's mind.

The last, and only, suspect on the list was Mr Hudson. He had the motivation to do whatever it took to make Rupert win the race as it meant that his house would win Sports Day for a record third year on the trot. *It has to be him*, thought Oscar.

Chapter Fourteen
A Marrow Escape

They had decided to keep up the guise of members of the press, but this time they were going to say they were freelance journalists as Mr Hudson would definitely know there wasn't a school paper.

As they rode over, Oscar cast his mind back to the last 'Teacher vs Student' rugby match. Essentially, it was a fundraiser but Mr Hudson had seen it differently. The game had started slowly at first, Mr Hudson barking instructions and shaking his fists at his other team members as if they were playing for the Six Nations not for the plastic medallions that would eventually be awarded to the winners. Mr Hudson had also invested in a special team kit for the teachers, all black.

Every time Mr Hudson got the ball, he would plough through the junior opposition as if they weren't even there, handing them off easily, with the children's faces being at the perfect height to be mashed by his hands. The score was already $121 - 5$ by the time the half time whistle had blown and half of the student team limped off; one of them was crying for his mum after a particularly hard tackle.

Whilst the students tended to their wounds, Mr Hudson had taken his team in to the locker room to give them a half-time pep talk.

"I think we need to let the kids score a few tries," said Mr Goff, the geography teacher. A comment he would regret immediately as he was quickly subbed.

"Show no mercy!" Mr Hudson had ended his speech with. The final score was 234 – 12. Mr Hudson had scored thirty-eight tries and committed three of the students to the nurse's office.

With that in mind, Oscar told Jude to bring the ninja spectacles in case there was any trouble. Jude was shaking so much he could hardly put them on.

There was an alley behind Mr Hudson's house so they had gone round the back to scope things out. Jude climbed up on Oscar's shoulders.

"He is in the back garden," whispered Jude back to his friend.

"What else?"

"He is watering some big cucumbers."

"Anything else?"

"He is talking."

"Who to?"

"The big cucumber I think."

Oscar lowered Jude down and told him to let him do the talking and make sure he got loads of photographs. They went round to the front of the house and rang the doorbell. It took a while as Mr

Hudson had to come in from the garden.

As he opened the door, the boys noticed he was cradling one of his prize vegetables. It did look like a cucumber but in fact it was a marrow not a cucumber and was wrapped in a blanket like it was a baby, swaddled like the baby Jesus doll they had at church for the nativity play. They both looked at each other as Mr Hudson led them through to the garden to the greenhouse. Jude did his 'he is mental face?' Oscar nodded his agreement.

"So, you've come to interview me about my Sports Day victory?"

"You mean Rupert's?" said Jude, without thinking.

"There's no I in team," Mr Hudson said as he gently laid his marrow back down on its custom-made plinth. Jude was trying to spell the word out, he did actually spell it with an 'I' but then spelling had never been his strong point. Oscar saw his chance to up the questioning, knowing that Mr Hudson was a sucker for a compliment.

"Well, he certainly couldn't have done it without you," he said.

"I try my best," said Mr Hudson, quickly adding, "for the kids, you know?"

Oscar nodded, trying to look serious.

"I guess getting ready for your big victory took a lot of planning. You must have prepared weeks in advance?"

Jude started taking pictures of the prize-winning vegetable.

"No pictures, please," Mr Hudson said quickly, "He doesn't like bright lights."

Jude was sure vegetables didn't have eyes but Mr Hudson was very insistent.

"So, can you tell us if you did anything special the night before the race? You know, last minute preparations."

Mr Hudson thought about the question intently, "No, I spent the evening with Percy."

Oscar wrote the word 'alibi' down in his notepad and slyly showed it to Jude, "And can Percy confirm this?"

At this Mr Hudson let out a strange high-pitched laugh.

"No of course not; he is a vegetable!"

"He is a what?"

Mr Hudson took them deeper into the greenhouse and at the far end there was an even bigger plinth than the one they had already seen, with even more first prize rosettes stuck all over the front.

"Meet Percy."

Jude and Oscar looked around; there didn't seem to be anyone in there. Jude nudged Oscar; he had spotted a name tag amongst the rosettes. Percy was Mr Hudson's prize-winning marrow.

Oscar crossed out the word alibi and wrote 'marrow escape' underneath it.

"Yes, I often water Percy late at night, he likes to listen to the radio too."

"You say you were 'watering' Percy?" asked Oscar.

Mr Hudson had drifted off into a fantasy about him and Percy going to Hollywood and making movies. He didn't know what the movies would be about, they just needed to have marrows in them; his marrow.

Oscar turned to Jude.

"Maybe he was watering something else?" he whispered.

Jude readied a ninja pose, patting his pockets down trying to remember where he had put the glasses. He nodded to the space below Percy where Mr Hudson stored a stack of watering cans.

Oscar pictured the scene; Mr Hudson pulling up in his car on the field. It was a cloudy night for a change and the shadowy figure of Mr Hudson was lit up by his head torch. He opened up the back of his van, which was full of the watering cans, and proceeded to soak the hundred metre track.

"So, no one saw you that night before the race apart from the marrow, I mean Percy?"

"Erm, no nobody but Percy."

"I see."

"Well, actually, yes, the photographer from the Bridlington Gazette. He had come to shoot mine and Percy's front cover," said Mr Hudson, proudly.

"These are very strange questions? What paper did you say you were from again?"

Oscar thought on his feet, "We are just so fascinated by Percy. Maybe we could come back and write a story about him?"

"I think we are done."

Mr Hudson looked across at Jude who was now in full strike mode, "Is he OK?"

"Jude? Yes, he's just never been a fan of vegetables."

The ride back to HQ seemed to go on forever. They stopped at a phone box on the way home and called the Bridlington Gazette and they confirmed that they had sent a photographer to Mr Hudson's house the evening in question. Now they really had nothing.

Rupert was in the clear, Rupert's dad seemed to have an alibi and Mr Hudson had been too busy serenading his marrow. Oscar crossed off the list of suspects leaving just a thread of red string leading to a big question mark drawn on the board. Jude had been quiet since they arrived back at HQ, obviously thinking about something.

"Do detectives eat sweets?"

"Yes, I believe they do," said Oscar.

Chapter Fifteen
The Paint Job

The sweet shop was that old, a bell still rang when you opened the door and as Oscar and Jude walked back out, it rang again. Oscar had gone for Lemon Drops, Jude had gone for the stickiest toffee he could find. Watson waited with baited breath, his tongue hanging slightly out of the side of his mouth in anticipation. Oscar casually tossed him a sweet.

Watson rolled it around his mouth for a bit. *Should have got Cola Cubes*, he thought.

The boys decided to walk back through the park. They didn't really speak; it's quite hard to have a conversation with a mouth full of sweets anyway. Jude had tried but his dribbling was out of control; he had tried to fit six bits of toffee in at once! They were so distracted they didn't even notice that they had left the park and were stood right outside Rupert's house.

Watson started to bark.

"Not now, Watson, you've had a sweet already!" said Oscar, assuming he was begging for more. But Watson didn't stop; he took a mouthful of Oscar's jeans and gave it a tug before running to the other side of the road.

Oscar and Jude watched him as he sat himself down on the kerb.

"It's Rupert's house!" said Oscar to Jude.

Rupert's dad's car was on the driveway, still really shiny considering it hadn't been cleaned the other night. The only mark was on the back wheel. The boys crept across the road and crouched down behind the bush that lined the front garden.

"Take a picture," said Oscar as he slipped out his spectacles and put them on. The lenses came alive and he quickly clicked his way through to 'Analyse' mode. The read out buffered as it processed the image. Once it was fully focused, the words 'white paint' appeared on one of the lenses.

"What is it?" asked Jude.

"It's our one and only clue," Oscar confirmed. "Quick, we have no time to waste."

They were running hard now. Jude was struggling to keep up, Watson was leading the way. They cut back through the park and made their way up the side of the school fence until they came to the hole.

"What are we looking for?" asked Jude, trying to catch his breath.

"This!" proclaimed Oscar as he pointed at the finishing line of the hundred-metre track.

"It's paint."

"Exactly!"

Oscar switched the glasses back to 'Analyse'

mode. The picture he took of Rupert's dad's tyre was still on the lenses. When he looked down at the paint on the hundred metre track the word 'match' appeared.

It was the same paint.

Back at HQ, Oscar was busy rearranging the evidence board. He placed the picture of Rupert's dad's car in the middle of the board, and then next to it pictures of: the large hole in the fence, the finishing line and a close up of the marked tyre.

"We've cracked it, Jude."

"We have?"

"Well, nearly. All the evidence points to Mr Walker, it's case closed."

"Great, let's go and tell your dad then he can go and arrest him."

"No, we go and tell Mr Rouse. He will know what to do," said Oscar as he gathered up the evidence and put it into his rucksack.

Chapter Sixteen
An Open and Shut Case

When they arrived at Mr Rouse's office, it was empty again. They walked back out the security door.

"Let's have a look around the back," said Oscar.

Behind the office, all they found were the bins. Jude leant against one of the bins, still exhausted from his run. As he did, a mechanised sound started up and the bins moved apart to reveal a secret passageway.

"Watson, investigate!" ordered Oscar.

Watson looked up guiltily. He had found a bit of sandwich under one of the bins, which had now moved out of reach when the bin moved. With one paw, he was trying to scrape it back into reach.

"Watson!" The dog pulled himself together and with his nose to the ground headed down the passageway. A moment later, Watson was back with Mr Rouse in tow.

"Gentlemen, follow me."

The two boys walked behind the old man. The passageway led to a long outdoor room shrouded in camouflage netting. At the end of the room were large pieces of cardboard with pictures of mean looking bad guys on them. The nearest one had what looked like bullet holes in it.

"Built this place myself," said Mr Rouse, proudly. "Completely soundproof."

"What is it?"

"It's my very own shooting range. I always like to test my spectacles before I give them to my special customers." He picked up a pair of glasses from the table next to him.

"Stand well back, please," said Mr Rouse as he ushered them out of the way.

He pressed a button on the side of the spectacles and a red beam shot out of them. The boys looked down the room towards the bad guys and could see the big red dot the beams had created smack bang in the middle of the cardboard villain's forehead.

"I think you are going to like this my fine dudes!" said Mr Rouse. He was far too excited really to be in control of a weapon. He pressed another button and two missiles, the same size as pencils, shot out of the glasses and flew down the room, totally destroying the target and promptly flying straight through the wall behind. Mr Rouse slowly removed the glasses.

"I think these might need a bit of work."

"That was so cool," said the boys in unison.

In the office, after they recovered the rockets from a tree behind the shooting range, Mr Rouse laid out the papers from the file that Oscar had pulled from his bag.

"This is good solid work," said Mr Rouse.

"Rupert told us that his dad had asked him to clean his car the morning of the race," started Oscar.

"But the hose disappeared," continued Jude.

"So, not only did Rupert and his dad have no way of sabotaging the track, Rupert was also with his mother."

"Rupert's one of us now anyway."

"He's in the clear."

Oscar paced one way and Jude decided to go the other. There was a good chance that any minute they were going to walk straight into each other.

"Then we went to the sweet shop. We go to the sweet shop," he repeated, detectives always repeated their statements on television.

"I had the toffee," interrupted Jude, "You went for the Lemon Drops."

Should have got cola cubes thought Watson.

"Anyway, on the way back we stop outside Rupert's house. His dad's car was on the drive. It was incredibly clean for an unwashed car, except for a splash of white paint on the back tyre," continued Oscar.

"The dog did a poo," Jude exclaimed.

"Not important." Oscar was on a roll. "It was exactly the same paint as they used on the sports field to mark the lanes out."

"Bingo bongo!" exclaimed Jude.

Mr Rouse agreed that the boys had a solid case,

the next step was figuring out how they were going to catch the criminal in the act.

"Do you remember I told you about my part in catching the Purple Claw?"

Oscar nodded.

"Mr Rouse almost single handedly caught the Purple Claw! Isn't that amazing?"

Jude had switched off; he had been trying to read the bottom line of the alphabet board. Oscar nudged him.

"Hey? Who? The Purple Claw?"

Mr Rouse tried to hide his disappointment. He had raised his leg up onto his desk, much like a proud explorer would at the top of a mountain, in anticipation of more praise. He awkwardly lowered his leg. Oscar could see the old man's feelings had been hurt.

"Please tell us how you caught the Purple Claw. If you think it will help."

He put his leg back up slowly, perched on the desk.

"Well...we knew who he was, the Purple Claw, but we didn't have enough proof to lock him up. So, we set a trap. We got the press to announce that a jewel, one of the biggest known to man, more expensive than all the money in the Bank of England, was going to be transported to the Museum of London for a one off show, knowing that he wouldn't be able to resist the temptation. Sure enough, he took the bait."

"So, we just need to think what will tempt Rupert's dad to commit another crime?"

Chapter Seventeen
The Trap

Oscar and Jude spent the next day in the library looking up traps. Jude was a big fan of 'Booby' traps because he thought it was a funny word to say. His first idea was to dig a big hole outside the Walker's house and cover it up with leaves so that Rupert's dad wouldn't see it and then fall in it on his way to work.

Oscar thought this suggestion might have something to do with Jude's outfit of the day, a safari number complete with hard hat and neck scarf. Jude had gone 'jungle'.

All the same, Oscar applauded Jude for his invention.

"There's one problem, we have to catch him in the act," said Oscar.

"We dig lots of holes?" suggested Jude. His cousins, Taylor and Lewis, were coming over at the weekend and he suggested that they would be happy to help out.

They looked at glue traps, snares and even beer traps. Oscar thought this would have been a good one to trap his dad as he liked beer, but they were mainly used for slugs and not to be confused with bear traps that were nothing like beer traps and had rather nasty spikes on them.

"We need to lure him out somewhere where we can then spring our trap," said Oscar.

"We could tie some string around a piece of cake, a really long piece of string, then just as he is about to get it we pull it away?"

Oscar liked this suggestion too.

"His crime was one of sport; he so desperately wanted Rupert to win the race he broke the law to do it," mused Oscar. "I've got it! We stage another race and this time the winner gets loads of money."

"But we don't have loads of money. I only get two pounds pocket money each week."

"It's just a trick to get Rupert's dad to sign up."

Jude screwed his face up and started to wag his finger at his friend.

"You are sneaky!"

The boys spent the afternoon making posters for the race. They decided to call it 'The Big One'. Underneath all the details they had written, Grand Prize £500 in much bigger letters. To avoid anyone contacting the school the fake race they said it would be held at the running track in the park next to Oscar's house.

"That will do the trick, I reckon," said Oscar, holding the poster aloft. "Rupert's dad will never be able to resist."

"Can I enter or am I too young?" checked Jude, still not quite grasping that the race was just a trick.

"Now we just need to stick these posters up everywhere."

They sneaked into the back of Jude's mum's cake shop to print off lots of copies and helped themselves to a few slices of cake at the same time.

Full of cake and armed with Jude's mum's staple gun, they headed out to put the posters up. By the end of the day, they had put up nearly a hundred posters, with most of them being stuck up on lampposts near the Walker's house. It was dark by the time they put up the last one.

"Now, we just have to be patient," said Oscar wiping his brow.

Jude stamped his feet; he didn't like being patient.

The next two weeks dragged by. The summer continued to heat up. The boys set the pool up in the back garden and spent most of the time with Oscar reading his favourite Sherlock Holmes, 'The Valley of Fear', to Jude and 'The Hound of the Baskervilles' to Watson.

Oscar had been crossing off the days on the kitchen calendar until the fake race and checking his mum's fake email account as he had put that on the bottom of the poster for runners to contact and register. No one would know it was his mum though as he had changed the address to u.bolt@yahoo.co.uk, thinking that might add to the attraction.

It had worked. The first day after they had put the posters up hundreds of people had already entered the race, but there was no sign of Rupert's dad.

Oscar decided to step it up a notch and got Jude to put on his ninja disguise and hand deliver one of the posters to the Walker house. They waited outside the house until Rupert's dad had gone to work and then Jude, with a mixture of commando rolls and a few punch-kick combinations, made his way across the front lawn and slipped the poster through the letterbox. Now all they could do was wait.

Chapter Eighteen
The Mystery Victory is Solved

It was the day before the race and the plan had gone like a dream. Rupert's dad had signed Rupert up and each morning Oscar and Jude concealed themselves in the bushes in the park and spied on father and son as Rupert was put back into his training regime.

Mr Rouse had spoken to one of his old friends on the force and he had agreed to come along as back up on the night prior to the race.

Oscar had butterflies in his stomach, Jude had Rice Krispies and Watson had some old sausages Oscar's mum had thrown out as they had gone out of date.

Oscar suggested to Jude that the red ninja outfit might be too much for a stake out and that maybe they should both wear all black so they could remain disguised. The plan was that the boys would have a sleepover at Oscar's house and, when everyone else was in bed, they would slip out the back door and rendezvous with Mr Rouse and his detective friend by the tennis courts in the park.

Annoyingly, Oscar's dad had said he was staying up to watch the 'Superbowl', the final of the American football season. It was on really late but his father would probably have quite a few beers so Oscar was pretty sure he would fall asleep before the game even started. He had thought about telling his father about the trap but was worried that he would put a stop to it all, and that Mr Rouse would get into trouble for handing out deadly spectacles to minors.

Oscar crept out of the room and waited silently on the moonlit landing for Jude to follow, but he didn't. He poked his head back into the room. Jude had taken the pillows and put them under the duvet.

"Now they won't even know we have gone," whispered Jude.

Oscar gave him the thumbs up.

It was still quite light as it was a full moon. Oscar liked those kinds of moons; when you could see the craters on the surface and make faces out of them. When they reached the tennis courts Mr Rouse and the detective were already there, sharing a drink from Mr Rouse's flask to keep warm. His friend was none other than Inspector Riley. The two boys immediately recognised him from the pictures in Mr Rouse's office. Both of them were wearing spectacles.

"Oscar and Jude, I presume. It's a pleasure to meet you. I hear you are great detectives in the making?"

Oscar and Jude couldn't really speak and it took them a moment to take the hand Inspector Riley had extended for them to shake. Oscar had a million things he wanted to say to the famous detective but none of them came out. Jude had never really shaken a famous person's hand so, just in case he broke it, he decided to just salute as he had become extremely good at it with all the practice over the last week. Watson just sniffed the detective's feet, quickly deducing that the man might be famous but also that he hadn't got any treats, *famous schmaymous,* he thought.

"Right, what's the plan?" asked Mr Rouse. They all crouched down. Oscar pulled out the map of the park he had drawn.

"So, over here," he said, tracing his finger along the map, "is a ridge where we can hide and wait for Rupert's dad to turn up."

Inspector Riley put his hand out and one by one they all put their hands on top of his, like the boys had done with Rupert.

"For Justice!" exclaimed Inspector Riley. "Remember, we need to catch him in the act."

They got themselves positioned on the ridge. All of them put their spectacles on and switched them to 'Night' mode. Oscar always thought night mode was like being dropped into a large glass of green juice on account of the green light. He also liked the way it made faces look and the little spots that flickered up like flames if the glasses picked up on any heat sources. He could hardly contain his excitement, although he was a bit scared too.

143

Jude didn't have night vision but he did have a really bright light on his digital wristwatch. He pressed it a few times to see how bright it was, putting his hand over the light making his fingers look all red.

It was getting colder as the night went on, the clouds had come over and only a sliver of the moon was showing. They had seen a few things through their night vision glasses: a fox, a badger and a security light which must have come on when the badger had got too close to it, but no sign of Rupert's dad.

"Can you hear that noise?" whispered Mr Rouse.

They all strained to hear it and sure enough there was a sort of grumbling noise coming from somewhere nearby.

"Where's it coming from?" whispered Inspector Riley, scanning the horizon.

"Could be a car approaching?" said Oscar. He turned to Jude; he was fast asleep and snoring. The others looked over too. It wasn't a car approaching; it was just a very tired boy. Oscar shook him lightly.

"Wake up, Jude, we're on duty."

He shook him a bit more. Watson stepped in and delivered a rather wet kiss on his nose. Jude was up and saluting.

"Try and stay awake," said Oscar, but he was interrupted before he could finish what he was saying.

"Quiet!" whispered Mr Rouse, raising his hand and pointing back to the entrance of the park; lights were approaching. They were car headlights. As the car pulled up next to the toilet block the lights were turned off. Everyone crouched down focusing on the hunched black figure that had emerged from the car and was now busy struggling to pull what looked suspiciously like a hose from the boot.

The mysterious figure switched on a head torch and headed to the outside tap by the side of the toilets.

"Switching to telescopic mode!" said Mr Rouse as he fiddled with the side of his glasses. Oscar followed suit. It took him a bit longer as he had never used that function before.

The strange figure was indeed Rupert's dad, although he looked to have rubbed black shoe polish, or mud, all over his face so it was hard to be totally sure. He was now pulling what looked like a rather new, fancy looking hose over to the hundred metre track. He placed the end of the hose in the middle of the track and then ran off back to the tap.

"Right, we wait for him to turn the hose on and then, on my command, we go," said Inspector Riley who was waving his fingers around in all sorts of directions giving instructions. Mr Rouse and Jude were to go one way and Oscar and Inspector Riley the other with Watson bringing up the rear. A 'pincer' movement as Inspector Riley put it.

They waited with bated breath, watching Mr Walker trying to grab the hose that had now started spraying all over the place. They watched for a moment longer as the man aimed the hose across the first five lanes.

"Right, go!" ordered Inspector Riley.

The detectives slowly made their way towards Rupert's dad, who was so distracted wiping his face, which had got wet when he lost control of the hose, that he didn't even notice them until he was completely surrounded.

"You're nicked!" said Inspector Riley, flicking his torch on. Mr Rouse did the same. Jude pressed the light on his watch. Rupert's dad dropped the hose, looking round at the assembled crowd.

"You can't prove a thing!" said Rupert's dad, "I'm just a local member of the community making sure the track is ready for the big race tomorrow."

"Actually, we can," said Oscar. "We have the paint on your car wheel which you must have missed when you washed it. It was a perfect match to the paint on the hundred-metre track at school."

"And we know the track was sabotaged before the race by someone soaking the grass," added Jude.

"I'm innocent."

"Then you won't mind coming to the station to answer a few questions?" asked Inspector Riley.

Rupert's dad was starting to look a little crazy.

"I won that race fair and square!"

"You'd better come with us Mr Walker." said Riley as he reached for his handcuffs.

"You'll have to catch me first!"

He turned and ran.

But he didn't get far.

What he had forgotten, in his panic, was that he was stood in a very large puddle where he had dropped the hose. He fell flat on his face in the mud.

A *fitting end for his days of crime*, thought Oscar.

Chapter Nineteen
Day Off.

Oscar and Jude had managed to creep back into the house unnoticed. Mr Rouse and Inspector Riley had walked them back to the end of the driveway leaving Rupert's dad locked in the car, sat on a bin bag so he didn't get mud all over the seat.

Victory feels good, Oscar thought as he climbed out of bed the next morning, his faithful partners still fast asleep. He walked over to the window and peeped out of the side of the curtains.

The road outside was lined with cars. In all the excitement of the previous night he had completely forgotten about the hundreds of people who would turn up for the race that day.

Leaving the other two asleep, he went downstairs and opened the front door. The whole road was full of very sporty looking people. There was even a lady using the front wall outside their house to stretch her legs out.

Oscar walked up to her.

"Excuse me, do you know what's going on?"

"It's the 'big one' today," said the woman, who

was dressed almost head to toe in Lycra. She handed Oscar a flyer. "It's big money too!" she said as she jogged off towards the park. Oscar opened it up. Maybe it was because he was sleepy, but it was only then that he realised it was the flyer him and Jude had made.

Oscar had meant to cancel the race once they caught Rupert's dad but it had been so late when they got back they had all fallen asleep before their heads had even hit their pillows.

Oh dear, he thought as he walked quickly back to the house. His mum was waiting at the door.

"What's with all the cars? Where's everyone going?"

"Some big race in the park," said Oscar cagily, wondering how quickly he could get onto his mum's email account and cancel everything.

"Ooh, another mystery to solve," his mum said, ruffling his hair as he passed her.

"No, not today." said Oscar, "It's my day off."